F

HATCHET JOB

HATCHET JOB

A Carl Wilcox Mystery

HAROLD ADAMS

WALKER AND COMPANY

NEW YORK

First published in the United States of America in 1996 by
Walker Publishing Company, Inc.
Published simultaneously in Canada by Thomas Allen & Son Canada,
Limited, Markham, Ontario

Library of Congress Cataloging-in-Publication Data
Adams, Harold, 1923–
Hatchet job: a Carl Wilcox mystery/Harold Adams.
p.   cm.
ISBN 0-8027-3286-0
I. Title.
PS3551.D367L38   1996
813′.54—dc20   96–24627
CIP

Printed in the United States of America
2 4 6 8 10 9 7 5 3 1

To my friend, Claire Hunter, faithful and frequent correspondent, who has brightened many a gloomy day.

Acknowledgments

My thanks and appreciation go to Barbara Mayor for correcting Carl's grammar and raising pertinent questions about story lines, and to Gail Myers, always a resource regarding life in the Dakotas back in the thirties.

HATCHET JOB

1

THE TOWN'S FIRST name was Mouseturd because of what the original resident found in his bedroll the night he moved in. He chickened out and changed the name to Mustard when the first woman arrived. Said he chose it because of the yellow clay banks nearby.

I got that story from Officer Schoop, who called me from Greenhill where I'd helped him in a little business a couple months earlier while in his town painting street signs.

Before I could ask how come he was paying for a long-distance call to give me that guff he asked how soon I'd finish the job I was on.

"What's the matter?" I asked. "You got another murder?"

"Not in Greenhill."

"So, it's in Mustard."

"Smart. You should be a detective. Fact is, this one's down your alley; a made-to-order Wilcox caper. I've talked with the Mustard mayor and he's ready to hire you as a temporary town cop."

"What happened to the last one?"

"Died of overexposure to an ax. Real messy."

"He have a wife?"

He sighed. "Right off you're looking for a widow, aren't you? Happens there is one. My sister. Some people think she might've done it. They hadn't been getting on for quite a while, but I know damned well she wouldn't have done this job. The killer worked her husband over from head to balls. It took more energy than Jackie'd spend on him."

I asked if they had kids.

"One boy. Mick. He's seventeen."

"Big for his age?"

"Average. I don't think he did it either. Lou Dupree, my brother-in-law, wasn't sleeping at home. Had a room upstairs in the City Hall, slept and got killed there. Look, this is costing me. I'd like to ask you as a personal favor, which you sure as hell don't owe, go take a look at this thing. Otherwise I'm gonna have to do it and there's nobody handy just now to take things over in town if I'm gone."

I remembered two great women in Greenhill and suggested I fill in for him while he went to Mustard. He said that was sweet of me but his sister being a suspect would make his involvement too messy so it called for an outsider with no relations as suspects.

I had to admit that made sense, asked him for directions, and agreed to take off after supper and look it over. I didn't promise to take the job.

"I figured I could depend on you," he said. "You don't have to mention me to Sis when you talk to her. First look up Mayor Tollefson at City Hall. Can't miss it."

That statement, which is never true in a big city, almost always is in a small one. Except, of course, the mayor wasn't in his office at 9:30 P.M., when I hit Mustard. I stopped at the hotel and asked for directions to the mayor's house.

The man behind the registration counter looked a week older than God but got to his feet spry enough and said I must be Carl Wilcox. He was thinner than my billfold, wrinkled as a fallen crab apple in November, and perfectly bald.

"Mayor Tollefson's expecting you—just drive straight west on Main, go two blocks, turn south on Third, and his is the white house on the southeast corner."

Tollefson answered the door and looked no more like a mayor than I do. The blond wavy hair, pale blue eyes, and dimpled cheeks would have been just right on a female Sunday School teacher. At five seven he even had to look up to meet my eyes when I moved inside and he led me into his living room. A slender woman seated in an overstuffed chair in the far corner looked at me with something short of admiration but smiled politely and offered her hand in a way that made me wonder if she expected me to kiss it. I shook it instead and flopped on the couch to her right as Tollefson parked in a chair opposite me after introducing her as his wife, Cornelia. Her hair was deep brown and drawn into a tight bun on her neck. From the size of the bun I suspected hair would hang to her waist when she let it down. I don't know why that sort of thing always gives me ideas. But then, I get ideas about most women not too young or too old and I've broad tolerance on the older side.

The mayor told me it was an awful thing that had happened in their town, the first murder in its history, and the bloodiest anyone in the territory had ever heard of. It had demoralized everyone and had to be solved quickly.

"Officer Schoop assured me you were the man to handle this job and we will, I assure you, give our fullest cooperation and support."

I asked how much it'd pay. He hemmed and hawed about and finally told me. I said I got paid better than that for being the town cop in Corden and there I saved money staying in my old man's hotel. So he made adjustments and told me I could use the room my predecessor had occupied. I nixed that and he conceded it was perhaps too much to expect, all things considered. He immediately suggested a boardinghouse and quoted rates, so it was plain he'd been planning and preparing all the way.

Naturally the boardinghouse he sent me to was on the opposite side of town from his. The woman running it was stocky as a hog but not as good-looking. She showed me to a clean room big enough to hold a bureau and a full-sized bed, while still leaving space for an easy chair in the corner. There was cross-ventilation and the windows were open with a nice cool breeze easing through.

"Can you cook?" I asked her.

"Can't you tell from the size of me?" she demanded.

"It's a good sign," I admitted, thinking of Bertha at the Wilcox Hotel, and agreed to take it. She said regular breakfast was at seven, and there'd be coffee and cereal if I slept late. She wanted a week paid in advance.

"What if it doesn't take me a week?"

"Hah!" she said.

2

TOLLEFSON'S WIFE HAD left the living room by the time I got back and the mayor was happy to hear I'd accepted the boardinghouse arrangements and started giving me the story on his late town cop. With no woman to distract me I took in the room, which looked like a setting for a Sherlock Holmes movie. The big lamps had tasseled shades, the carpet was lush and full of fancy designs that'd hide anything you dropped but an open ink bottle. We sat near each other, me in the corner of the heavy couch, him in a giant morris chair that made him look like a teenage prince on a throne. Between us one of the big tasseled lamps threw light that got lost in shadows in the far corners of the wide parlor.

He asked if I knew Lou Dupree had been living in an unfinished room over City Hall since he split with his wife? I said yes, Schoop told me.

He nodded. "Lou'd been there a little over three months when he was murdered. Worked nights, mostly. Supposed to be on duty till dawn but I suspect he retired by two or so since nobody's up after then anyway. Weekdays he always showed up at Albertson's Café around nine and wasn't officially on duty till

7:00 P.M. but you know how it goes in a town our size. He was actually on duty twenty-four hours a day, seven days a week.

"Sundays he mostly loafed. Last Sunday he wasn't seen after dark. Monday morning he didn't show up for breakfast at the café and I got a call from Albertson, the owner, asking if I knew what was going on. I sent a man over to check Lou out. He found the door open, called, went inside, and found this bloody mess on the bed in the corner of the room. I can't give you details on that, you'll have to talk with Doc Pelham. He examined the body."

"Was Dupree dressed?" I asked.

"I told you, I don't know any details. Don't want to know things like that. It's none of my business. You talk with Doc Pelham."

"Why'd Lou and his wife break up?"

"I gather it was mostly over the boy, Mick. Lou was an old-time first sergeant in the war and heavy on discipline. Mick was, let's say, independent."

"Where was the boy Sunday night?"

"I don't know. I can't tell you where Jackie was either."

"Officer Schoop's sister."

"That's right."

"Who else was sore at Lou Dupree?"

"Well, as a matter of fact, just about anybody in town. Lou had a talent for rubbing folks the wrong way. I couldn't name one person in town he could call his friend."

"Was he a woman chaser?"

"I couldn't say."

The tone made it plain he could if he would and at the same time let me know I'd have to get my details elsewhere.

"How'd you like Lou?" I asked.

That got me a cool look but after a second he decided not to take offense, for the moment.

"I felt he was a very capable officer and kept matters in hand most efficiently."

"I didn't ask about how he handled his job, I wondered if you liked him personally."

"I respected him. You should know he was a strong character who suffered severely in service—lost most of his company in combat—and it marked him. I've thought a lot about Lou and pretty much come to the conclusion that his experiences in the war made him afraid of getting too close to people so he had to hold back. It was as if he had the notion that personal attachments made a man weak. Lou was fanatical about being strong. I don't mean physically, but morally and spiritually. It twisted him."

"He a church man?"

"Went every Sunday. That, I understand, was one of the family conflicts—Jackie's not a spiritual woman—goes to church on special occasions and didn't believe Mick should be forced to attend Sunday school. Lou did and Mick went till he was about grown up."

He squirmed around in his big chair and leaned toward me. "I think I should make something clear. I want you to talk to folks in town yourself, get your own impressions fresh. I don't want you getting prejudiced about anybody because of something I might say."

I resisted the impulse to ask why he'd be prejudiced against anybody and just nodded.

It was after eleven when I left him and went back to the boardinghouse. The front door was unlocked and I went up to my room without seeing anyone. The house was perfectly still when I went to sleep.

About 6:00 A.M. a clattering in the kitchen woke me and I managed to crawl out and get decent by seven so I was able to get the whole breakfast of buckwheat cakes, bacon, eggs, milk, and coffee. I learned the boardinghouse owner was called Aunt Leck but still don't know why.

The other boarders were elderly, as usual, except for a blonde

Norwegian named Yvette Hamsun, who I guessed was in her early thirties. She was careful to avoid direct eye contact but I caught her sneaking a peek and tried to look soulful instead of flirty. It worked okay. By the time we were almost through eating she responded with a little smile and headshake when I asked if she was related to Knut Hamsun, the Nobel winner.

"Read his books?" I asked.

Another headshake. "They don't have him in our library." Her eyes finally met mine squarely. "Have you read him?"

"Nope. They don't have his stuff in the Corden library either."

"Somehow you don't strike me as a reader," she said.

"Oh, I take a crack at it now and again. You a teacher?"

She flushed slightly. "Does it show?"

"Just a lucky guess. I'll try another—you're not from around here, are you?"

"No. Fargo, North Dakota. That's where I was born and went to school."

"My sister lives in Redford, a ways north of Fargo on the Red River. I was up there a couple weeks last summer."

After some polite chatter about that she got up, and I walked out of the dining room with her. She stopped at the foot of the stairs and when I paused beside her, wished me luck in my new job.

"You know what I'm here for?"

"To find out who killed Officer Dupree."

"How long have you been teaching here?"

"Two years. I'll start my third this fall."

"Did you know Dupree?"

"Yes."

"Well?"

"I wouldn't say that."

"Know if he had any friends?"

"No, I don't, but what you're really interested in is, did he have enemies, isn't it?"

"You can learn a lot about a man from either," I said. "Since you and I are both outsiders in this town, it could help me to know what you learned about since you moved in."

"I'm not great at gathering or spreading gossip," she said. "I deal mostly with children and, happily, they seldom talk about grown-ups, not even their parents. Now I'm going upstairs. I'm sorry I can't be any more helpful."

I watched her go up and suspect she moved with special care to avoid interesting hip movement but that's not easily controlled and hers was fine enough to give a man dreams.

Aunt Leck came out of the dining room, caught me admiring the scenery, and snorted.

"You don't waste time, do you?" she said.

I gave her my warmest smile and said not if I could help it.

"Who told you she was involved with Lou Dupree?" she demanded.

I managed to keep my chin from dropping, dug up a grin, and said, "You just did, Aunt Leck. Tell me more."

"I've told you too much already. You want more, you'll have to get it from her—and I suspect that's just what you'd like."

You can't beat women for understanding.

3

I WAS INSTALLED as town cop a little after ten Saturday morning and then Tollefson said I should meet some people and we set off for a tour of the business district while he outlined my responsibilities. It pretty much boiled down to staying in sight, checking for locked doors after closing time, breaking up fights in the beer parlor and pool hall, and keeping a sharp eye out for fire hazards, roving gypsies, and vandalistic schoolboys. And of course I was to check out parked cars where spooners might be going too far.

We stopped first at the Widdifelt Hotel and I learned the ancient I'd met at the desk the night before was Bert Widdifelt, the owner. In the daylight his head looked like a wrinkled skull but there was nothing dead about the blue eyes or the broad grin.

"You don't take after Elihu," he told me after shaking hands. Elihu's my old man, who runs the Wilcox Hotel and is about the last man I'd pick to take after. I asked where they'd met. He said at a shindig in Aquatown for people in the hotel business.

"That was before he got all busted up in that auto accident. How's he doing?"

"Had a couple strokes since then. Getting by on pure meanness the last I saw him."

Bert chuckled, shaking his head. "Good-lookin' old man," he said with open envy. "Finest head of white hair I've ever seen. And the squarest hands. Had a grip like a blacksmith."

"They're still strong," I said, "but the legs are shot. How's business?"

"Awful. Gettin' worse. I make it to hunting season I'll get through another winter but then I'll try to sell or just close up."

"How'd you like Lou Dupree?" I asked.

A little uneasiness edged into the blue eyes.

"Like? All right, I guess. Lou wasn't a friendly man. Did his job, kept the peace. All you can ask of a lawman."

"Why'd anybody kill him?"

Bert glanced at Tollefson and they exchanged innocent blue-eyed stares. "I don't know. Only thing comes to mind is somebody mad because of the way he treated his family and the way he worked on just about any woman in town. Still, it don't seem enough to make anybody I know go crazy with an ax."

"Whose women did he work on?"

"Well now, I don't really know . . . just heard some talk . . ."

"About who?"

"Well," he glanced uneasily at the mayor, "I heard he was trying for that schoolteacher, Yvette Hamsun, and I guess there were others. . . ."

"Any attractive woman, young or old," said Tollefson. He tried to make that casual but it came out heavy.

I glanced at him, wondering if I should ask how Lou acted toward the mayor's Cornelia but decided against it.

"Who else was interested in Yvette?" I asked.

Bert chuckled again. "About every buck in town, I'd say. But she's not easy to reach. Doesn't go to the Saturday night dance or let fellas take her to the movies and sure wouldn't go flivver riding with anybody."

"When we hire a teacher," Tollefson told me, "she is given

a clear understanding that her deportment must be exemplary."

"That mean the only place she can meet guys is in church?" I asked.

"That's where she met Lou," said Bert, grinning.

Tollefson made a show of looking at his watch and told me he had an appointment with the city attorney and would have to leave me on my own.

"Maybe," he said to Bert, "you could take Carl around and introduce him to other businessmen?"

"Sure thing," said Bert. "I can get Paula to watch the front."

Tollefson said he'd talk with me later and left.

"You want to start around now?" asked Bert.

"In a minute. How long've you run this hotel?"

"About a dozen years."

"You born here?"

"Nobody was born in Mustard seventy-two years ago. Didn't have a county formed till 1882. No, I come from the old country just before the Great War. Got my citizenship and enlisted the same month. After I got out I came here because I had three brothers farming over near Corden. Worked with them a year, got married, worked up a partnership with the brothers, and started this hotel. Been here since '24."

"Okay. Let's go over to the café and have some coffee while you fill me in on things. I'd like a little advance dope before we move around."

He called his wife in from a room beyond the stairs, introduced us, told her importantly that he was helping me in my investigation of the Lou Dupree murder, and we went down the shimmering street a block to Albertson's Café, picked a booth next to the kitchen, and settled in.

Lou, he told me, had been a hotshot athlete in high school, played football, ran in track events, and starred on the basketball team.

"He was only five ten," said Bert, "but in the three years he played center nobody ever outjumped him regular. Lou was all quick and mean. They called him Elbows Dupree. We had a really stinky coach back then, taught all the dirty tricks in the book and made up more of his own. I'd guess Mustard had the most unpopular team in the conference and Lou could take most of the credit. I figure that's what maybe spoiled him. I mean, he believed sneaky cheating was the way to win. And being a star made him real popular with girls and that made him cocky. He married our cutest cheerleader, Jackie, and everybody figured he'd do big things but he didn't ever get anywhere and wound up the town cop."

A fat man came out of the kitchen and stopped by our booth. Bert introduced him as the owner of the café, Ken Albertson. Ken's face was pumpkin round, pink-cheeked and blue-eyed. He said he was pleased to meet me like he really meant it, shook hands, wished me well in my work, and said I'd find it worth my while to try one of his meals as a change from Aunt Leck's table.

"From all I hear," he said, "she's not a bad cook but doesn't offer much variety. Of course I got to admit I don't often have any people in here quite as pretty as Miz Hamsun except on Sundays when she comes in for supper."

"She eat alone?" I asked.

He glanced at Bert and back to me.

"Did at first. Last few weeks, Lou Dupree happened by and joined her."

"Just since he left his wife?"

"In the last month, I'd say."

I looked at Bert. "You said a while back there might be people sore at Lou for the way he treated his family. What'd he do to them?"

"Well, some thought he was cheating on Jackie, and they knew he whipped the boy pretty bad."

"Whipped?"

"I don't know as it was real whipping, more like he slapped

him up and maybe punched a little. And one week Jackie had a black eye and other times bruises. On her forehead and cheeks. Maybe other places—who knows?"

"The mayor ever get on him about that?"

"If he did it wasn't in public."

"He'd never done it anywhere," said Albertson. "The mayor figures a man's home is his castle and he's in charge."

Bert admitted that was probably right.

We moved on and I met the banker, who watched me so close I suspected he'd heard about my holdup and rustling record and figured I was planning a bank job next. I looked his place over good to keep him on edge and tried to remember any banker I'd liked. I decided my favorite was the one who'd killed himself. One of his workers told me the boss pissed ice water. I figured he wasn't all cold-blooded if he couldn't face his customers after the bank failed and lost their money. Others might think different, but I couldn't believe any man would rather be dead than broke.

4

B Y N O O N W E had hit the bakery, hardware, drugstore, grocery, and butcher shop. Merchant reactions to the killing ranged
from the baker's indignation about such a bloody murder happening in Mustard to an almost joyful fascination with it all by
the butcher. A few of them were nosy about me, others held back,
as though embarrassed that a stranger was poking into private
lives in their town.

I told my guide it was time to eat. He took me to the Nordstrom Café, across the street and south of Albertson's.

We sat at the counter and ordered choices from a woman he
called Doris. Her grin wasn't the warmest I've seen but seemed
natural enough and she didn't hang around to gab.

I asked Bert who Tollefson sent to check on Lou when they
got curious about the cop not showing up Monday morning.

"Colby Link, guard on Lou's basketball team. Got crippled
up in a car accident his senior year. Does odd jobs around
town—real handy with tools. Learned about electricity in the cities.
Old Colby can fix anything from cars to a door latch. Doesn't
want to work steady for anybody so he just freelances around."

We found him in Tollefson's backyard, changing oil in the

mayor's Oldsmobile. He finished the job before paying me any attention, then wiped his hands on an oil rag and lit a Camel while peering at me with dark suspicious eyes. His bare arms were brown and wiry, he was slightly stoop-shouldered, which almost hid his barrel chest. His chin was like an anvil—a real knuckle buster. It was plain he hadn't had a haircut since spring and wasn't too handy with a razor.

"This is Carl Wilcox," Bert told him. "He's supposed to find out who murdered Lou."

"How're you gonna do that?" he asked me skeptically.

"Any way I can. You got any ideas?"

His eyes didn't waver as he scowled at me. Finally he took a deep drag on his cigarette, let it out, and shook his head.

"None of it makes sense. He hadn't been near the wife or kid in weeks and even if he had, neither of them'd use an ax. It about had to be somebody crazy, hacking him all up like that."

"How many times was he hit?"

"It looked like a million, but the doc says four. Balls, chest, neck, and head. Blood all over. Messier'n hell."

"Any signs of a fight?"

"What the hell, I told you—blood all over!"

"But the rest of the room, anything knocked over. . ."

"Nah."

"So he must've been caught asleep."

"Uh-huh. He was bare-assed except for a slipper on one foot. I figure the other flipped off when he got hit the first time. It was on the floor at the foot of his cot."

"Was he a drinker?"

"Well, sure, who don't?"

"So he could've been drunk."

"Could be. Doc said he hadn't had supper."

"What'd you do when you saw the body?"

"Hightailed down the stairs and back to Tollefson. He got the doc and sent him over."

"Anybody see the body there but you and the doc?"

"Fred Hicks. The two of us put Lou on a stretcher and hauled him over to the doc's for the autopsy."

"Was the room locked after that?"

"Uh-huh. Tollefson had me put a padlock on it."

I thanked him and asked Bert to take me to the doctor.

Doc Pelham lived on the south side, not far from Tollefson. He too had a corner lot and there were tall pines flanking the front walk. His office was in a downstairs bedroom, very neat with a heavy curtain separating it from a small dining room. He had a desk and examination table, white cabinets built along one wall, and a linoleum floor with a black-and-white check pattern. We caught him between patients and he lounged in his leather upholstered swivel chair while we sat in straight-backed wooden jobs that put us in our proper place.

Doc Pelham looked tall and lanky even sitting down. His white jacket draped over a bony frame, his eyes were deep-set, brown almost to black, and peered from under trim beetled brows. The cheekbones stuck out and his jaw was long and sharp edged. Skin sagged on his neck except where it stretched over his Adam's apple.

"The facts are brutally simple," he said. "He'd evidently been drinking quite a little beer but hadn't consumed any drugging agent. He'd been struck four times. Once each to the head, neck, abdomen, and groin. Each blow precisely centered. The navel was split, the nose struck exactly between the brow and tip, and so on. Death from the head blow must have been nearly instantaneous."

"Can you tell which was the first target?"

"Most likely it was the head or neck because the body would naturally double if the first blow was to the groin or abdomen, preventing clean blows to the head or neck."

"So whoever did it wasn't just hacking like crazy."

"Certainly not. The blows were deliberate, calculated, and powerful."

"About what time you think he got it?"

"Probably near the middle of the night, give or take two or three hours. These things can't be pinpointed."

"How'd you like Lou?" I asked.

His heavy eyebrows arched. "Like? I had no particular feelings toward him. Saw him almost every day. Why?"

"Trying to figure what people thought of him. So far it seems he wasn't exactly a favorite citizen. You married?"

"I am. And if you're implying my wife could have been involved with Lou Dupree, forget it. She's at least fifteen years too old for the man and has never touched an ax in her life."

I grinned at him. "How about you, ever use one?"

He glared like I was a cockroach he'd found in his soup. "Tollefson said you thought you were funny. He doesn't think so and neither do I. No, I've never handled an ax. I'm not even particularly adept with a scalpel. Is there anything else you want to ask?"

I said no, thanked him for his time, and we left.

Bert shook his head as we walked along under the sun.

"How come you asked him if he'd used an ax?"

"When he told about the chopping job he took more than a little satisfaction in the way it was done. Made me wonder."

5

I ASKED BERT to show me where Lou's widow lived. In front of her house I thanked him for all his time and suggested he drift back to his hotel while I visited with her. He wasn't too pleased with that and walked off looking sour.

She answered the door so promptly she must have been standing behind it when I knocked.

Jackie Dupree was my favorite type: small and curvy with mahogany-colored hair brushed to a gloss, dark brown eyes, and long black lashes. Her skin was tawny and I caught the scent of talcum powder, which beats all perfume for me. Her gaze was direct and friendly as a cat facing the neighbor's terrier. I could imagine how it would raise the hackles on a macho man like her late husband.

"You're the man the mayor hired in Lou's place," she said. That came out like an insult and I admitted it was true.

"I suppose you think I killed him?"

"Haven't jumped to anything like that, no. Just like to hear about him from you. Might help me settle this thing."

She pushed the screen open, but instead of letting me in, came out on the porch where two wooden rocking chairs, weather-beaten and creaky, stood side by side. She sat in the nearest one, leaving me to step past her and take the other.

"Lou," she told me, "was a complete SOB. I suppose, to be generous, it wasn't all his fault. His father was a sanctimonious judge and his mother was a ninny and in school he was such a hotshot athlete he thought that made him forever special and never got over the fact it didn't mean pooh once he graduated."

"They say he beat you."

"That's a lie. He hit me when he got mad. And then only once except when he didn't catch me good with the first swing. I never believed in making it easy."

"What'd he get mad about?"

"I think it made him mad to be awake, but anything to do with Mick aggravated it. Wanted him to be an athlete just like his dad and of course it never worked out."

"Mick wasn't interested in sports?"

"No. He's a student. Real good in math and all that. Very ambitious. Last year he tried to start a delivery service with another kid in town—they bought a used truck and were going to deliver groceries and other stuff all around. Only there just wasn't enough business and buying the truck on time put them in the hole from the start and finally Lou had to bail them out. He was sore as hell about that. Said Mick made a fool of himself, getting big ideas. Now Mick works part-time for Bert at the hotel mornings and evenings and in the afternoon does deliveries for the grocery store."

"Didn't that impress his father?"

"Lou said he was running his tail off for pennies. Which is almost true—but people respect Mick and he respects himself, so why not?"

He sounded a little bit like my nephew Hank, only not as smart.

"Folks also claim Lou beat him."

"That's another lie. If he had, I'd have killed him. He used to spank him too much when he was little and they had one fight when he was about grown but after I laid into Lou about that he never hit him again. I told him flat I'd kill him. And don't let that give you ideas, because I never had cause. However I despised Lou, I had no reason to kill him. We were separate, he didn't come around bothering me, and he left Mick alone."

"I hear he messed with other women."

"Of course."

"You make it sound like that didn't bother you."

"When I first got wise, I told him to get all he could away from home because he'd never have me again."

"You didn't care if he slept with other women?"

"I was tickled to death. As long as he did that I could tell him to go to hell when he wanted to mess with me. I'd rather have slept with a dog."

"Because he was unfaithful?"

"Yeah," she said with sarcasm that made it plain her dislike went further than any shortage of talent in the sack.

I rolled a smoke and fired up before asking another question. She had watched me closely a second after answering the last one and I felt she guessed that I was wondering if her disinterest in sex with Lou was him or the business itself. So I switched directions.

"Was he supporting you?" I asked.

"Lou?" Her laugh was bitter. "I support myself. Got a job at the five-and-dime four years ago and this spring became the manager. That's the real reason Lou moved out. He couldn't stand being married to a woman working steady and making it. I don't make anything like I told him I do, but it puts groceries on the table and coal in the stove. Lou quit making payments on the house two months ago. I sure wouldn't help myself any by chopping him like kindling just because of that."

"You going to give up the house?"

"Probably. We'll see. I want Mick to go to college in Brookings and it isn't likely I can keep payments up and handle that at the same time."

"Did Lou leave any money?"

"I hear he had twelve dollars in the pockets of pants he left laid across the chair by the cot. We'd only been paying on the house six years so it's not close to clear. Maybe there was a little in the checking account. I haven't seen the book since he left home."

"From what I hear," I said, "it sounds like your boy might manage to take care of his own way."

"He'd like to," she said. Her face changed at the mention of her son. All the hard mean went. She turned soft and warm.

"I've got to ask you some nasty questions," I said. "Don't get the notion I'm just nosy or nasty—but when things went bad between you and Lou, didn't you look for something else yourself?"

The warmth cooled. "I thought about it. But in a town like this it'd get known overnight. I'd have to worry that Lou might kill anybody I got even friendly with, and just as bad, I'd get talked about and that'd hurt Mick. I couldn't let that happen. It was bad enough him having a father who made a fool of himself chasing all the tail in town, although most of these fools thought that was all right. But a mother fooling around, that'd raise pluperfect hell."

"How'd Mick feel about his dad?"

"Oh, Lord, he was all mixed up. There were times he hated him but at the same time he was almost desperate to have his approval. I'll admit, that made me mad. I tried not to show it and think mostly I managed but of course when Lou moved out it was clear I couldn't stand him. Mick had some trouble with that but in the long run, understood. He's a good, sensitive boy. Too forgiving, if anything."

"How'd he handle the murder?"

"Better than I expected. He worried about me. I could tell

he was afraid I'd feel guilty. I had to fake a little to keep him from seeing what a relief it was. I won't lie. I didn't shed a tear. Never will. I was a damn fool to marry him, there wasn't a good day in the whole marriage, and all I'll ever regret is that I didn't break up with him sooner."

"How come he moved out of your house? It doesn't seem the guy I've been hearing about would let you have it."

She looked out across the yard, beyond the tree-shaded street and at the houses facing us.

"He surprised me on that. My argument was that Mick needed a home and a mother and the only way he could have both was for Lou to get out. If he didn't go, I would and I couldn't even afford rent for a decent place. Lou was a lousy father but he did have enough decency to accept that. Or maybe I'd been bitchy long enough by the time he went that it was a relief moving to that room over the City Hall. And it had a fire escape in back where he could bring tramps in and could roam as he pleased. He never cared what he ate so losing my cooking didn't matter."

I asked if she knew anybody who particularly hated Lou.

"Oh, you've got a broad choice there. The old man who brought you here, Bert, is one."

"Why?"

"I'm not sure. Something strange happened at the hotel one night about a year ago. I wasn't talking with Lou by then and never got the story clear. There was a woman guest and I suspect somehow Lou got involved. You'll have to ask Bert."

"How about Doc Pelham?"

She glanced at me sharply and smiled.

"What in the world made you think of him?"

"He enjoyed telling about the corpse a little more than seemed natural."

"Well, aren't you clever. Yes, Doc's another who hated Lou. It started when I had my appendix out over two years ago. Doc did the job and Lou claimed he charged too much and said it loud all over town. And Doc was very nice to me. When I told him about my ambitions for Mick, he offered to give me a loan and I was dumb enough to let Lou know. Lou went over and gave him what for— accused him of trying to buy me. It was pretty messy."

"Anybody else?"

"Probably dozens I haven't even heard about. If I think of any, I'll let you know."

"Where's your son?"

"Upstairs. Why?"

"I'll have to talk with him."

"He can't tell you anything I haven't."

"Come on, you can't know everything he does. We might as well get this over with right now. I'll go up and see him."

"I don't want you alone with him."

"Look, I'm not going to give him the third degree. Wouldn't you like it better if I talk to him here than at City Hall?"

She stared at me for several seconds, sighed, and said, "All right. Let me go up and tell him you're coming and why."

"Don't try to rehearse him," I said. "It won't help anything."

"Don't worry."

I knew she wanted to be sure he didn't contradict anything she'd said and decided what the hell.

"Go ahead," I said.

She gave me a small, appreciative smile and went up.

6

JACKIE WAS GONE several minutes and apologized when she came down, saying Mick was upset about talking to me and she needed time to reassure him. She looked relieved when I waved that off.

"His room's the second on the right at the head of the stairs," she said.

I climbed up, walked to the open door, and looked into a small room with a single bed, a bureau, desk, small bookshelf, and a clothes rack in the corner. It was neat enough to make me suspect his mother had done some picking up and straightening during their talk. Mick was lounging on the bed with pillows stacked behind his head. He wore corduroy slacks, a blue shirt, and striped socks. His shoes were on the floor, unshined.

I pulled a straight-backed chair clear of the desk and sat facing him. If he was upset he hid it well with a typical teenager's bored look. His mother's talk about him not liking sports made me expect a lightweight but he was strictly solid.

His complexion, except for a forehead pimple, was his mother's, the hook nose and square jaw were all his own.

"You don't look like any cop," he said.

"You don't look like a student," I said. "I'm sorry about your dad."

"Why? What's it to you?" He looked mad.

"I said I was sorry because that's what you do when you talk to relations of anybody killed. It doesn't make me a phony mourner."

He thought that over and the mad look faded.

"You got any idea who might've killed him?" I asked.

His eyes met mine. "I've tried to think about it and I can't. Don't want to. Is that nuts?"

"It's probably pretty smart. Not likely to make you feel any better. From some of the things your mother said, I got the notion you wanted your dad to like you. She got that right?"

"She overdoes it," he said and looked down at his striped socks.

"When's the last time you saw him?"

He scowled. "That's funny, I been trying to remember. Since he left here, I mean. I'd see him every now and again in town—in a place like Mustard you can't hardly miss the cop any day. But I can't remember seeing him all that last week and don't know for sure when was the time before that. Maybe in Albertson's, or on the street. Why?"

I grinned at him. "To see how you'd answer. You talk with him any after he moved out?"

"No. Well, I take that back. I did. Three months back, when he stopped making the house payments. I told him what I thought of that."

"Where were you at the time?"

"That room he worked from in City Hall. I went over there and told him I thought it was lousy."

"What'd he say?"

"He said he didn't feel like he'd ought to pay for any place he wasn't living in and he thought his kid ought to be smart enough to understand that."

"Did you?"

"Well, sort of."

"Were you surprised he didn't get mad?"

"Yeah." The admission seemed to bother him. "When he was home if I'd said that he'd have belted me one."

"Did you figure all the trouble between your parents was your dad's fault?"

"Well, sure, wouldn't you? He was the tomcat and bully. So maybe she did yell a lot there toward the end."

"So maybe you didn't blame him for belting her."

"Well, in the last couple years he didn't do that. Hell, he wasn't around much."

"Did you see him with other women?"

"I saw him eating supper at Albertson's with Miz Hamsun."

"But that was after he'd moved out of your house, wasn't it?"

He lost interest in his socks and stared at me.

"Yeah, right. I didn't see him with any women before that. He was too sneaky."

"You hear any stories from kids at school?"

"Yeah," he said with disgust. "For years."

"Think for a minute. Were there any women you heard about that had husbands or boyfriends who might've got hot at your dad?"

"Hell, just about everybody in town. From old Nordstrom, through Doc Pelham and even the mayor. It's be easier to name people who didn't have a special reason to be sore at him." His expression was no longer bored, the memories of humiliation were too much.

"How about people your dad jumped on as a lawman? Anybody that might've carried a grudge?"

"He broke up fights at the dance hall a couple times and got rougher than hell with guys who wouldn't listen when he tried to make them back off. I didn't know any of them too well, except Wes Fox. Dad put him down real bad one Saturday night a couple years back and it made Wes sore as hell but he's a crazy guy who'd never hold a grudge."

"Tell me about it."

"It was kind of complicated. There's a first cousin in Eureka Dad knew pretty well whose daughter came to the dance because she was kind of stuck on a trumpet man with the band playing here that night. She came with a couple other girls. The band guy didn't have any time for her and pretty soon Wes worked up to her and got her to go out for a ride in his car and was parked on lover's lane when Dad drove around and found them. I think somebody'd warned Dad that Wes was kinda fast and might get her in trouble. Anyway, Dad pulled up beside them and jerked Wes out of the car—"

"What's the girl's name?"

"Lettie Dupree."

"Okay, what happened?"

"Well, she didn't have all her clothes on and Dad lost his temper and whopped Wes hard enough to give him a black eye. He looked pretty bad for near a week. So of course everybody gave Wes a hard time. Old Wes, he just laughed them off."

"Wes still in town?"

"No. He went to Aberdeen last fall. Works for a plumber there."

I asked Mick if he had a girlfriend. He turned red as a gas can, shook his head, and avoided my eyes.

"How come?"

"They only like guys that play football or basketball, or talk a lot."

"You're looking at the wrong girls," I said. "The flashy ones are usually nothing but grief. Try the quiet ones. It makes them grateful."

If the suggestion inspired him any it didn't show.

"You take any classes from Miss Hamsun?" I asked.

"Uh-huh. English."

"How'd you do?"

"Got an A."

"She a popular teacher?"

"I guess so." He was very casual with that.

"What makes her popular?"

"Well, she's the youngest woman teacher in school and the girls think she's an angel and the guys go for her. She makes classes interesting."

"You surprised your dad was having supper with her?"

By this time his expression was more guarded. He sat up on the bed and hugged his knees.

"I didn't understand it at all," he said. "Why'd she eat with him?"

"Maybe he just sat down to talk with her and ask about you. Ever think of that?"

At first he looked startled, then I got a scornful look that could have shriveled a more sensitive soul.

"No," he said, "I never thought of that. It's a dumb idea."

I said maybe so, and after a couple seconds asked where he'd been when he heard about his father's murder.

His face lengthened, he blinked once and said, very low, "At the grocery, making up an order. Ma came in and told me."

"Where'd she hear?"

"Mayor Tollefson came to the house and told her."

"Where were you Sunday evening."

He said he'd been home and looked me in the eye when he said it. I thanked him and left.

Jackie must have been listening for me because she appeared as I reached the foot of the stairs.

"Well, satisfied?" she asked brightly.

"Pretty much. Think he had a crush on his English teacher?"

"No," she said a little too quickly. "Girls have always frightened Mick. Women terrify him."

"He ever get an A in English before?"

"No. She was just the first teacher who made him think English was important. Mick's not the kind for crushes. Never."

I thanked her and drifted toward the door. She followed. Before opening it I faced her again.

"Didn't your brother tell you anything about me?"

"Al?" she said.

"Yeah, he's the cop in Greenhill, in case you don't know. Asked me to take this job. Don't you talk with each other?"

"No, we haven't been close since I married Lou. Al thought it was dumb of me and said so. We haven't been close since. How'd you know him?"

"I helped out some on a murder in his town not long ago."

"So," she said, suddenly smiled and I thought was going to laugh but it passed. "Well, he was worried about me. Just like Al to send help but not even call. I guess I'd better call him."

I said that was a good idea and looked back at her through the screen. "Where was Mick Sunday night?"

For less than a second she studied my eyes, then said, "Here. With me. We were both home all evening."

I nodded and took off.

7

I FOUND ALBERTSON behind the counter of his café and told him we had to talk. He nodded, led me to the booth near the front window, and took the side with the street view.

"You here the Sundays when Lou ate with Miss Hamsun?"

"Always around," he said. His pumpkin face made it hard for him to look serious but he worked at it.

"They sit in a booth?"

"Uh-huh."

"Ever come in together?"

"Nope. She'd show first, he'd come in, look around, walk over, and ask did she mind. She'd just tilt her head and he'd park."

"How'd they talk?"

"Quiet. Not whispery, but privatelike."

"Any notion what was going on?"

"Well, there was no hand-holding or leaning close. He did most of the talking. She pretty much watched her plate; he mostly watched her. It wasn't lovey-dovey, you know? More like real serious. Like he had things to tell her."

"How often did that happen?"

"Four times. Each Sunday before the one he got killed."

"She come in to eat that day?"

"No, she didn't."

"How about Lou, he come around?"

"Uh-huh. When he didn't find her, he walked out."

I asked if the waitress at the counter was the one who waited on the couple and he said no, that was his wife, Sue. She didn't work Sundays. Ella Parker was the one. If I wanted to talk with her I'd have to wait till Sunday because she was in Aberdeen today.

"You know Wes Fox?" I asked.

"Oh, sure. He's the reason Ella's in Aberdeen. Her folks live there and she goes to visit them Saturdays so she can see Wes at the dance in town. They're probably gonna get married this fall."

I went back to the boardinghouse and asked Aunt Leck if Miss Hamsun was in.

"Why?" she demanded.

"I want to ask her some questions."

"I can imagine the kind. She's not here."

"Aunt Leck, I'm the town cop, I get to ask questions and people are supposed to answer. Where can I find her?"

"At the library."

"Where's that?"

"Upstairs in City Hall."

"That's where Lou Dupree was staying?"

"His room was down the hall from there."

I found the mayor in his office and said I wanted the key to the room where Lou was killed. He said fine and handed it over.

"I hear," I said, "the library's up there too."

"That's right. Open Saturday morning and evening and on Wednesday evenings."

"Who's in charge?"

"This summer it's Miss Hamsun."

"Well, well," I said, and went up the stairs.

It was nearly 4:00 P.M. by then and thinking the library might not be open much longer I passed the padlocked door and went on through an open door at the end. Miss Hamsun was standing by a girl in her early teens next to a shelf along the east wall and glanced up as I entered. She said something to the girl and stepped toward me.

"Yes?"

"How much longer's the library open?" I asked.

She glanced at the clock on the wall and said five minutes.

"I'd like to talk with you when you're free. I'll be in the room Lou used down the hall. Would you stop by?"

She said yes.

The room smelled stuffy and looked bleak as a good priest's sex life. Except for little details like black blood splattered all about, it was orderly as a marine barracks. There was a three-drawer bureau against the west wall, a nightstand by the cot with a goosenecked lamp and a copy of Sinclair Lewis's *Ann Vickers* beside it. In the northeast corner a fishing rod leaned against the wall over a tackle box and a dark green knapsack. The one window was high on the west wall and only needed bars to make the place look like a cell. I stared around, trying to picture the killer coming in with an ax and asked myself, how'd the doc tell whether it was an ax or a hatchet? Maybe he assumed it from the penetration, but anybody handy could manage the job with a sharp hatchet. I opened the drawers, pawed through underwear, shirts, and socks, and found only a two-cell flashlight and a Milky Way candy bar.

As I was shoving the last drawer closed steps sounded in the hall and Miss Hamsun looked through the door.

"Did Lou Dupree come around to see you when you were working up here?" I asked.

"Only once," she said. She took one horrified glance at the cot where Lou died and switched her complete attention on me.

"When was that?"

"The day before he was killed. Do we have to talk here?"

"Where'd you rather?"

"Let's go in the library. I'll close the door. I don't open up again until seven."

We went back and I parked in a straight-backed chair next to her desk while she settled in the swivel job with her knees hidden under the desk. Her hands gripped the chair arms.

"What do you want to know?" she asked.

"What Lou talked to you about at Albertson's."

She shifted slightly, crossed her legs, and settled against the chair back.

"The first time it was his son, Mick. He said he was worried because they couldn't get along and he blamed his wife for turning the boy against him. He said since I had lots of influence on him maybe I could make him see his father wasn't evil and only wanted him to make the most of himself."

"What'd you say?"

"I told him I didn't think Mick would pay much attention to my opinion of their family relationships even if I were presumptuous enough to try and intrude."

"That was smart," I said. She gave me a suspicious look, trying to decide if I was on the level, then went on.

"He agreed that might be a problem and asked would I mind if he told me a little about himself so I'd know all the problems weren't just his fault and that all he wanted was what'd be best for his boy."

She paused again, watching me close. I nodded.

"I said he gave me credit for more influence than I thought I had but if he wanted to talk about it I wouldn't mind listening. So instead of talking about himself, he went on some more about Mick. Said he was full of high-flying notions of getting rich at the same time he was a mama's boy and didn't think he should ever get paddled and when he was, no matter for what, stayed sullen for days. I think what bothered him most was Mick didn't like fishing with his father or playing catch or anything else like that."

"How'd the talk go the next Sunday?"

"He got around to himself."

"He talk any about people he had trouble with outside of his family?"

"Nobody in particular. It was mostly that nobody understood him and people in general had it in for him."

"I noticed the book on Lou's nightstand was from your library. Know why he picked it?"

"I recommended it, thinking it might do him some good."

"Did it?"

"I don't know. He checked it out the Wednesday before he was killed and I never spoke with him again."

"You didn't go to Albertson's for dinner that Sunday, right?"

"No. Four times was too many, people were beginning to talk. And besides, I was tired of his troubles."

"He hadn't maybe started coming on a little too strong, huh?"

"There was that too," she admitted.

"You told him you wouldn't be eating there Sundays anymore?"

"I didn't think I owed him explanations. I knew he'd figure things out if I didn't show."

"Were you afraid of him?"

She stared straight into my eyes for several seconds before answering, "Yes. He seemed more like a man who'd kill than one who'd be murdered."

"Why?"

"He was full of hate. All the talk about his son and wife, and other people in town. When you listened closely, after a while, it was very plain. He hated them all."

"You too?"

"Everybody."

"Didn't Dupree's kid give you any trouble?" I asked.

"Not a bit. We got along fine."

"Maybe that was Dupree's real gripe. He figured his kid was falling for you."

She smiled.

"I've been wondering," I said, "about you staying in Mustard through the summer. Most teachers can't wait to get out of town the minute school closes."

"Most have families to return to, or summer jobs to carry them over. I don't, so when they offered me the library job and Mr. Tollefson persuaded Mr. Jenson, owner of the weekly newspaper, to put me on as a proofreader and do some writing, I jumped at it. Mr. Jenson thinks he can get me on the paper in Aberdeen next summer."

"You going to be a sob sister?"

"I suppose it'll start that way, but I hope for more."

———

WE WALKED BACK to City Hall after supper and she went up to the library while I parked in the office and thought about murder.

8

LATER I RETURNED to the library and asked Yvette why she'd recommended the book *Ann Vickers* to Lou Dupree.

She gave me an embarrassed smile.

"Because it was written by a man from a woman's point of view. That didn't make it as good as something a woman would write on the subject, but Lewis worked very hard to give the woman's side and he showed more understanding than most. I suppose it was a silly idea and doubt Lou ever looked at the novel."

"There was a bookmark about a third of the way in."

"That's not necessarily significant. He might only have been planning to impress me."

"I think maybe you felt sorry for him."

"Yes, I guess that's true, I did. Much of the time there was this kind of panic when he talked, as though he might suddenly lose control and scream. He'd put his hands on the table and clench his fists until the knuckles turned white. I don't believe anyone I've ever known talked through clenched teeth the way you read about, but he came close."

"What'd he talk about?"

She folded her hands on the desktop and twisted them

slowly. "It mostly came down to feelings. Needs, hates." She paused a moment and finally said, "Passion. He said I didn't show anything but calm. That to look at me a man would think I didn't have any feelings at all, no fears, desires, or warmth. Actually he said 'heat.' "

"That bother you?"

"Yes. I resented it very much. I think he used the word 'heat' deliberately, to get a reaction."

"Heat, as in bitch?"

She blushed and nodded.

"You think he was trying to scare you?"

"Yes. It was his way of dominating. He had to make an impact. He couldn't impose love or affection, but he could arouse fear. That gave him the only satisfaction he got with me. I can't help thinking he would've felt some perverse thrill over being killed by a person he'd inspired to such hate."

That was a little deep for me but I must have looked impressed because her shy smile surfaced and she quit twisting her hands.

"I'm talking a great deal of rot," she said.

"He ever get down to propositioning you?"

"No. He skirted it, I suppose, and would've been direct if I'd given him any encouragement at all."

"Is that why you didn't show up at Albertson's that last Sunday, when he was killed in the evening?"

"Yes. He'd been building up to something the Wednesday before, when I pushed the *Vickers* book on him. I was a little surprised he took it. Most of all, I was grateful that there were other people in the library nearly all evening. We were only alone a very few minutes."

"He talk about other women?"

"Only his wife. And he only talked about her the first two Sundays. He was sensitive enough to know that bothered me. I mean, him talking about her. He gave too much away."

"About what, their sex life?"

She blushed and nodded. "He said she didn't have his passion or needs, was a cold fish."

"Anyone else in town come on to you?"

"Wesley Fox did a couple times. When he was still around. He hasn't been here more than once or twice since last year."

"You date him any?"

"It was never exactly that. Wes is way too young for me but he's a weird combination of things, very bright boy, clown, wit, and loads of fun. Almost impossible to put off. He coaxed me into seeing a movie with him once. Claimed he needed me to explain the significance. Another time he talked me into going to the Saturday night dance. I can't believe I did that."

"Bert Widdifelt told me you never went out on dates."

"Bert just thinks he knows everything that goes on."

"I'd like you to do me a favor," I said.

"What?"

"Go to the dance with me tonight, after work."

She studied me for a moment. "I've a feeling you're asking me for more than the usual reasons."

"You're right. I want to see the reaction of guys that show up at the hall. Find out who's interested and what they make of it."

That wasn't a complete lie but of course it wasn't all the truth either. She gave me a knowing smile.

"All right. At nine we'll go back to Aunt Leck's, I'll change, and we'll go to the dance. Just don't expect too much."

"I never expect much, but I'm a great hoper."

9

IT WAS HOT in the open and stifling in the dance hall despite a giant fan mounted in the corner over the bandstand. Doc Boone's Band was pounding out the Hut-Sut song with more enthusiasm than talent and couples were making the most of it when Yvette and I drifted in. There was some open gawking but mostly just carefully casual peeks and a little nudging and whispering among the seated girls and the standing guys. Yvette smiled at me, moved to the dance floor, and turned, raising her arms.

I do a hitch step or a walk to any beat the band plays and nobody ever stopped dancing to watch me and my partner put on a show. The walk is nice for snuggling and the hitch usually keeps me on the beat. The Hut-Sut was for the hitch and Yvette followed well enough to make me feel like I wasn't too bad. I worked her around to the side of the hall away from the rubberneckers and she said nothing until the number ended. As we stood waiting for the band to get organized for the next piece, she leaned close.

"I thought you wanted to watch reactions," she said.

"Had to get into the beat first, didn't want to embarrass you."

She looked knowing and raised her arms again when the band started something new to me.

"What do you think of reactions so far?" she asked, speaking into my ear as we danced.

"About what you'd expect. Now we see how many of these guys have guts enough to ask you for a dance."

"I doubt there'll be that much interest. The young boys are shy and the older ones don't expect much from a schoolteacher."

To my surprise, she was right. When we drifted back toward the wallflowers and the daisy pickers no one edged our way, male or female. All we drew were quick peeks and sneaky glances. Just as the band started a new set I noticed a sudden flurry at the entrance and a red-haired young man appeared with a blonde in tow and drew greetings, calls, and waves from several of the dance crowd. A few stags and couples moved to meet them.

"That's Wes Fox," Yvette said.

"The lothario our late cop socked?"

"The one."

He had an easy grin, an arrogant jaw, broad shoulders, and a politician's way with the handshake, shoulder pat, and light touch.

"How big was Lou Dupree?" I asked Yvette.

"About a match for Wes."

The redhead's eyes worked the crowd until he spotted Yvette and his grin widened. Then he glanced at me and while the smile hung in I thought I caught a change in the eyes. A measuring, thoughtful look.

"Let's dance," said Yvette.

We went through the next three numbers and she warmed a little with each one. The body contact was something past cozy and my rising hopes couldn't have been any secret to her. I wanted to believe she was getting carried away but suspected she was putting on a show— most likely for Wes.

When we walked off the dance floor Wes was waiting with

his sunshine smile and asked if she'd have the next with him. She said no.

"The one after?" The smile didn't waver.

"I'm all booked," she said.

"Don't tell me," he said in mock alarm, "you're in custody?"

"You can call it that."

He looked at me and grinned. "Okay, this is Wilcox, the murder man who's supposed to solve the case of the finely chopped cop, right?"

"Right," said Yvette, "and now we're going out and find something cool."

His expression became sober and sincere. "In case you've heard otherwise, it's not true I'm engaged."

"That's none of my business," said Yvette.

He suddenly grinned again. "After dancing with you a man needs cooling," he said, and tilted his head my way. "Watch yourself, she teaches all levels."

Yvette smiled kindly and we moved off.

The outdoor air felt lovely and the wind seemed almost cool for the first dozen steps.

"What do you want?" I asked as we stepped around a family of farmers chatting in the center of the sidewalk.

"What I'd really like," she said, "is a cold beer and a cool swim."

"Sounds good. Where?"

She shook her head in frustration. "Nowhere in this town. If we went into a beer parlor, by noon tomorrow, if not before, everybody'd know the schoolteacher/librarian had been swigging beer and I'd be back in Fargo. Not that it doesn't seem like a good move sometimes."

"Do people ever swim in that puddle west of town?" I asked.

She looked at me for a second, then nodded. "Yes. Kids go out there. The water's clean, it's a spring-fed, which means it's a little cold but there's sand along the southern edge I understand."

"You game?"

"We'd have to go back to Aunt Leck's for my swimming suit. Have you got one?"

"Yup."

"Will you behave?"

"I'll try."

She laughed and we turned off the city street and headed for the boardinghouse. She told me this was absolutely crazy but she had a feeling if she didn't let go once she'd bust.

"I get so tired of living like a nun," she said.

We got in without seeing Aunt Leck and met in back where my Model T was parked. I cranked it to life and we wheeled out and headed west. There was no moon but stars were bright enough to make the earth glow. The road jogged around the swimming hole and we pulled off the gravel and onto packed earth near a row of box elders and one large cottonwood.

When I turned the engine off we sat a moment, looking at the star-reflecting water a little ways below and hearing the frog chorus all around. She twisted on the seat and looked about.

"Do you see any place you could put the car where it wouldn't be obvious from the road?"

"In the pool, if it's deep enough."

She laughed nervously. "I really wouldn't mind getting fired," she said. "I like teaching but my luck's been too good. Nothing but kids I really care about. I'm bound to get a bunch of stinkers one day and it'll be spoiled. What I'd really hate would be going through the mess of denunciations and bitterness involved when you disappoint people."

"You think too much."

"That's what Lou told me. So did Wes. You men never have to think. You don't experience what we do, no matter what happens."

That was so plain it didn't call for talk but she was hurting so I admitted she was right. It didn't seem to comfort her any.

"Well," she said, "we came to swim."

We got out, peeled off the outer duds and walked a little apart toward the water. I went in up to my knees, she stopped with just her feet in the still water. I could see her white legs, slim and smooth. Her waist was neatly tapered, her breasts small and high. She looked at me, not taking her eyes from my face.

"You were right," I said, "it's cold."

She nodded and waded forward deliberately, letting the water rise over her thighs, hips, waist, and chest, never pausing, then plunged forward and began swimming carefully with her head up, trying to keep her hair dry.

I dove in and came up a little ahead of her. Her teeth gleamed in the starlight as she smiled.

"Isn't it fine?" she whispered.

We swam side by side to the far side. The bottom was beyond toe reach and the bank sloped too sharply to climb so we started back. I felt things were too fine, a car was certain to pull up loaded with drunks. Why would anyone stay stinking and sweating in that oven dance hall when they could be here?

After a while we waded out of the water on the beach near the car and I gave her one of my two towels and used the other while watching her. She moved without awkwardness or self-consciousness. When she was dry she handed me the towel and I draped it over the car hood beside mine.

"Have you got a blanket?" she asked.

I got the army blanket from the trunk, stretched it out on a sloping plot of grass, and we sat down. Our suits felt damp and cool, the night breeze was warm and gentle. The frogs croaked on in the slough east of us.

We got pretty involved after some preliminary kissing and touching and when it was clear it was going to get really deep she told me she wouldn't do it without a rubber.

"Well, hell, I haven't got one."

"Bring me my purse from the car," she said.

I don't think I'd been much more surprised if she'd taken wing and was tempted to ask if she also had a bottle in the purse. It took some rummaging but she came up with a rubber and handed it to me still in the wrapper.

"Don't get the idea this is something I do every week," she said. Her voice had anger in it; she was defensive and beginning to withdraw.

"You've got good sense," I said.

"It seems so damned cold-blooded, but I am not going to get pregnant."

"It's okay."

"Listen, I'm going to tell you something before we do anything more, okay?"

"Okay."

"The first time I ever made love I got pregnant. I had a baby girl. She lives with my older sister in Fargo, and calls me Aunt Yvette. The father was just a nice dumb kid. It was all my own fault, I was romantic and stupid and thought I had to know everything and do everything. I've been gun-shy ever since but lately I've been thinking about doing this more and more and when I saw you I knew this was going to happen and I wanted it to and I got the rubber through a cousin who's very understanding. Now please don't hurry or get rough, all right?"

I said all right and only had trouble with the "don't hurry" business but am lucky enough so too soon doesn't mean goodnight and finally I was getting her to tell me what she wanted and it went real good considering I kept thinking about our vulnerability on that damned beach. Okay, so I didn't keep thinking about it all the time because she got pretty involved in telling me what was good and I followed all the directions with a few variations of my own and only fell short of never stopping which was something she mentioned about forty times. When I did stop she didn't complain any, which made me grateful.

I can remember women who complained that I just used them and this was my first experience with feeling like the used instead of the user. It didn't offend me any. In fact it made me a little proud. At the time I thought I wouldn't mind getting used as often as a toothbrush.

10

AS WE HEADED back to town she leaned against me and asked if I would go to church with her in the morning.

"I'm not much for church."

"I'm not either, but I go for other people. It makes them feel more comfortable about me teaching their kids and running their library."

"Why bring me in?"

"Because it'll just about stun the town and they'll go nuts figuring out what it means. The word will be around about Yvette Hamsun being at the dance with Carl Wilcox and leaving early to go God only knows where, and coming in late. Then they see us together at church and it'll mess them up something awful."

"Okay, we'll go."

She kissed me on the ear and said I was terrific.

When we had left the car and started around to the front door she stopped me.

"Have you got a suit?"

"Yeah, but it's not much."

"And a tie?"

I admitted I did. It was a concession I'd made in taking the cop job in Mustard. I knew at one time or another I'd be expected to look like a real citizen so I came equipped with stuff borrowed from my old man, Elihu.

She laughed and told me again I was terrific and she'd kiss me again if she weren't afraid Aunt Leck would be watching through the front window.

I expected the old lady would be waiting up to meet us but there was nothing but a small lamp on in the parlor and a smaller light in the upper hallway. We parted at Yvette's door and I went on to my room and hit the hay. There's no sweeter sleep than what you get after a cold swim and hot loving.

Next morning we went to the Methodist church and I warmed to the minister on sight. He had a flattened nose and kindly crinkled eyes. I caught him looking at my busted beak with a secret grin and later wasn't surprised that his sermon carried more quiet assurance and comfort than fire and brimstone.

We filed out with the crowd toward the minister, who'd got to the entrance while we finished the last hymn and was laying in wait for handshakes and blessings. The mayor, trailed by his bun-haired wife, edged close and remarked on how pleased he was to see me here. A little ahead of us I saw Albertson, and looking around spotted a few characters who'd been at the dance the night before. Wes Fox wasn't among them but the blonde he had been with was. I nudged Yvette, who leaned close, and asked her who Fox had brought to the dance. She whispered, "Ella Parker. She works Sundays at Albertson's."

The parson gave me a warm hand and a firm grip, which delayed me while he said how happy he was to have me in his church.

"Your predecessor was a faithful member here for many years, I hope we can expect the same of you."

I thanked him, smiled my dumbest, and moved on when he let go. Yvette, who was enjoying the whole business, lagged on the walk, offering and accepting greetings from citizens who drifted close to look us over and consider the meanings in this ritual.

When we were clear of the crowd she laughed and hugged my arm.

"That was wonderful," she said. "I can't thank you enough. They're absolutely out of their minds over this whole thing."

"I must be thick," I said. "I don't get it."

"These people have put me in a little box for the past two years, thinking I was a doll woman, with no past, no interests outside of the classroom and library. I was a nothing. Now they realize maybe I'm real but they can't begin to decide a real what. I love it."

"You want me to go to the pool hall tomorrow and tell them how real you are?"

"You wouldn't do that, would you?"

"Hell no. I'd have to fight every man in town—if they knew what I know every one of them'd be after you."

"They'd probably want to burn me as a witch."

"The women, maybe—but none of the men."

"Oh, Lord, you don't know these men."

"I know them better than you do."

Aunt Leck didn't serve Sunday dinner to the boarders so I suggested we drift around to Nordstrom's. Doris waited on us and I paid her close attention. I guessed her at about forty years. Her body was a little heavy but with slender ankles, a tapered middle, and impressive superstructure. She was taller than average and moved in a deliberate, no-wasted-motion style. The chin line was beginning to relax some, she had small wrinkles at the corners of her mouth and eyes that showed more character than age.

It seemed to me she could probably swing an ax or a hatchet handily.

When she delivered our meals I asked if Lou Dupree had eaten here often?

"Fairly. After he split with his wife. Ready for more coffee?"
I nodded and as she poured, asked what she thought of him.
She pulled back the coffeepot and studied me a second.

"What kind of an answer you expect to that?"

"If I knew, I wouldn't ask."

She glanced at Yvette, who looked uncomfortable and nudged my ankle under the table.

"We weren't rivals," said Doris.

"Yvette thinks he hated women, maybe everybody. You ever think that?"

"Your schoolteacher reads too many books. She never began to know Lou Dupree. He was a poor, mixed-up, sad son of a bitch that nobody understood. Not his kid, his wife, or anybody else."

"Except you."

"I understood he was screwed up. But he wasn't my problem and I can't tell you anything about who killed him, let alone why. You going to have dessert?"

"We'll see."

She left us.

"You shouldn't have asked her about him in front of me," said Yvette.

"Maybe not. I'll try her another time."

"She hates me."

That was one of the things I was starting to learn but there didn't seem any point in telling Yvette that.

I asked if she felt like going swimming again when we were walking away from the restaurant. She laughed and said no, on Sunday there'd probably be kids out there and she thought that would take away the charm.

"You ever gone to the Lutheran church?" I asked.

She glanced at me. "Yes, why'd you ask?"

"Bert told me you met Lou in church. I wondered if it was his or yours."

"I don't belong to either. I go to one and then the other, depending on my mood."

"When Wes Fox came around last night, what was that business about him not being engaged?"

She looked a little flustered but tried to hide it.

"It was nothing."

"Is he supposed to be engaged to Ella Parker?"

"So they say."

"Why'd he think you'd care?"

"I can't imagine. I never gave him any reason to think that'd be of the least importance to me. Just because I let him talk me into a movie and one dance doesn't mean I ever let him get any big ideas."

"I suppose you've heard that story about how Lou knocked him around once for messing with Lou's cousin?"

"I overheard something about it once. Why?"

"Well, it explains why Wes can talk about Lou's murder pretty lightly. He'd be especially happy, I suspect, if he knew Lou had been shining up to you at the Albertson café Sundays. You ever get any idea Wes might be bad jealous?"

"I think he's perfectly normal."

"Why'd you put him down so sharp at the dance?"

"Because I've outgrown him. I think I knew it from the beginning but it took you to make me realize it."

That was supposed to throw me off and it did for several minutes before I started thinking seriously about Mr. Fox.

11

BEFORE SHE WENT up to her room I asked Yvette where Ella Parker lived.

"With her aunt. It's west aways, you'll have to look up the address in the phone book. Under Patience Parker."

I fed Aunt Leck's pay phone a nickel, told the operator who I wanted, and two rings later was talking to Ella Parker's aunt, who was suspicious until she understood who I was and then turned hostile. I laid on polite respect a foot deep and eventually got her to tell me Ella was somewhere downtown with her fiancé, Wes Fox. She had no idea where and thought things had come to a pretty pass when the police started hunting innocent girls.

I allowed it was a cruel world and assured her Ella wasn't about to get the third degree or find herself thrown in jail.

Patrolling Main Street twice didn't turn them up so I drifted over to the Widdifelt Hotel looking for the town gossip, Bert, and found his wife gabbing on the telephone behind the registration counter. She looked at least fifteen years younger than her husband, which still put her some past ripe. Her short hair was gray and her teeth had been made by a dentist who was more willing than artistic. Still the smile was warm and her blue eyes watched me alertly as she listened to a distant voice. Finally she said yes while nodding, and hung up.

"Looking for Bert?"

I said yes, she said sit, she'd get him.

She scuttled through a doorway behind her and I parked in an old rocker and lifted the Sunday paper from a broad table under a big pendulum clock on the wall.

Mrs. Widdifelt came back, said Bert would join us in a moment, moved around the counter, and took a rocker opposite me.

"Well," she said, "how you like Mustard by now?"

I was tempted to say only on hot dogs but squelched it and said I liked it fine.

"You think Jackie killed her husband?"

"Why'd I think that?"

"Because he whaled her and their boy and wouldn't make the house payments."

"Would you chop Bert if he treated you like that?"

"I'd more likely use the cleaver than an ax."

"Figure no jury'd hang you, right?"

"Right. Lou was no saint, you know."

"Tell me about it."

"You must already heard plenty. It was no secret."

"What'd he do here?"

"What makes you think he did anything here?"

"I heard Bert hated Lou over something that happened in the hotel."

"Well, who'd tell you a thing like that?"

"Probably about half the town."

She laughed and Bert came through the door behind the registration desk and asked what he missed.

"Ask him," she answered.

Bert took the rocker on my right, started stoking up a stubby black pipe, and gave me the raised-eyebrow look.

I dug out my makings and built a cigarette while telling him what I'd asked his wife. His eyebrows came down and about met over his nose as he scowled like a Halloween mask.

"With all due respect for the dead," he began, "that son of a bitch accused me of running a bawdy house. There was this Amelia, a chubby blonde gal from the East who stayed here summer before last a week or two. Now I don't pertend she didn't flirt with fellas and swing her hips wicked and maybe wear more paint than a drunk circus clown, but she never brought fellas into the hotel and up to her room like he claimed. Never, not once. You know why he got all in a tizzy about her? I'll tell you why. Because when he got fresh with her she cut him deader than old fish. That's all there was to it. She hurt his precious pride is what she did. He couldn't stand that and told me I had to throw her out and I told him to take a running jump in a dry lake and he threatened me and by God I went to the judge and got that business straight."

"What was the lady's business in Mustard?" I asked.

"She called herself a hair stylist. That's what a hair dresser calls herself when she charges an arm and a leg for work. She took a room saying she wanted to look the town over to see if she might set up a shop here. She'd run one in Chicago, had some bad experiences, and decided she'd be happier living in a nice small town where people cared about each other and the men behaved themselves. When old Lou proved all the bad guys aren't in big cities she just gave up and moved on."

I glanced at his wife, Paula, while Bert talked, and caught her watching me closely like a naughty kid listening to a friend tell his parents a whopper.

"You kind of liked this Amelia?" I asked Bert.

"Of course, everybody but Lou did. She was real nice. Treated us like grandparents, didn't she, Paula?"

Paula's face turned instant innocent.

"A real nice girl," she said, nodding.

"What was her last name?"

"Parradine."

"She talk with anybody in town about buying or renting space for her shop?"

"Sure," said Bert. "Visited lots with Mayor Tollefson and Mr. Springer, our banker. They own quite a bit of Mustard real estate. Both talked with her more than once. They liked her too, I'll tell you. A real sprightly gal."

"You have any other troubles with the town cop?" I asked.

"Well, he was messing around with Mae Olson, one of our hired girls, for a while but it didn't last. She was real young and kind of stunned about getting a rush by the town cop. I guess maybe he thought she was too easy."

"How long ago was that?"

"Oh, golly, what was it, Paula, five, six years ago? Something like."

I thanked them for their time, butted out my cigarette in an ashtray on the newspaper table, and stopped at the door.

"What do you think of Ella Parker?"

"Ella?" said Bert. "Fine girl, feisty as a fox, quick as a squirrel."

"Think she'll marry Wes Fox?"

"Well now, the question is, will Fox marry her? There's no telling about that boy—he's slippery and wild. Ella'd be smarter to pick another but she's got her cap set for Wes and she usually gets what she wants."

I looked at Paula and asked what she thought. The mischievous look was back on her face.

"Well," she said, "the fact she's got everybody in town thinking she's engaged to him ought to tell you all you need to know about Ella Parker. At least it should if you've ever taken a look at her ring finger."

"Bare, huh?"

"You got it."

12

WHEN ANOTHER SASHAY around town still didn't turn up Wes and Ella, I checked Nordstrom's home address in the phone book and gave a call early in the evening. Doris answered and told me her husband had gone to bed early—wasn't feeling good.

So I swung around to the widow Dupree's house. The second she met me at the door I guessed she'd talked with her brother. She invited me inside like I was Santa arriving with a full bag, offered coffee, and wanted to know if I'd like a piece of cake with it. I never turn down anything a woman offers and haven't often regretted it.

"I guess you called Brother Al," I said as she delivered the coffee and cake.

"Uh-huh. He told me never to let you in the house when I was alone."

"Where's Mick?"

"Out somewhere."

"You always ignore your brother's advice?"

"Always. How'd you make out with the schoolteacher?"

"Learned quite a bit."

She gave me a grin as she sat down, crossed her ankles, and cradled the coffee cup on her knees.

"I keep hearing what a great teacher she is. But I suspect she could learn a thing or two from you."

"She says Lou was full of hate."

"Really? I'm surprised he'd let her know. I didn't see any of that until after we were married. Maybe that says something about me, huh?"

I ate cake and drank coffee for a few minutes. The cake was a devil's food and about good enough to sell your soul for, with a rich reddish cocoa body and a light fudge frosting nearly a quarter of an inch thick.

"You think Lou managed to get her to bed?" asked Jackie.

"No. She was afraid of him."

"So she told you."

I finished the last of the cake and drank the hot, strong coffee.

"What do you know about a blonde woman named Amelia who came to town a couple years ago and stayed a week or so at the hotel—supposedly planning to open a beauty parlor?"

Jackie's eyes opened wide, and then she laughed. "Who told you about her?"

"Bert. What's so funny?"

"That whole episode. You should've seen her. One glance and you'd figure if she was going to open anything it'd been a brothel."

"She was selling it?"

"She sure as the devil advertised it. The clothes she wore, the way she walked. Men followed her around drooling. It was disgusting."

"Was that what you got from Lou?"

"I saw her myself, I never got any of my opinions from Lou, believe me."

"You know Lou accused Bert of running a bawdy house?"

"Of course. He let everybody know it. I never believed that but I know one thing, if Bert had been running one with her in the stable, Lou'd have been the first customer. He'd loved to have been her pimp."

"So why'd he jump on Bert?"

"Because she put him off and Lou wanted Bert to give her the boot. Did Bert describe her to you?"

"Some. He admitted she was a little showy."

"That's putting it mildly."

"Who'd she get cozy with in town?"

"Well, she saw a lot of our mayor and the banker. Supposedly for business reasons. The story was that she wanted to rent a shop downtown. She actually did Amanda Springer's hair one afternoon, at home."

"Who's she connected with?"

"Our banker, Philip Springer."

"Who else did Amelia talk to?"

"Well, I understand she and Colby Link had a few conferences. The story was, she'd be having him fix up her beauty shop with cabinets and things. Some say she encouraged him more than was fair; him being a cripple."

There was some more talk on that subject that didn't add much and finally I asked if she'd talked long with her brother and she admitted, almost shamefaced, that they'd gone on about forever.

"He really always meant well with me," she said, "he just didn't have sense enough to know he couldn't tell me what to do."

"How'd he happen to say something about not letting me in your house when you were alone?"

"He was only kidding. Said you had quite a reputation with widows—almost as bad as your record of carousing and fighting."

"Was that it, he just knocked me?"

"No," she smiled. "Don't ever let on I told you, but he's very impressed. Told me not to underestimate you. Said it was easy to do but a big mistake. Coming from him that's something special. He doesn't impress easily. Do you like him?"

"Yeah. He's all right. A lot smarter than about any other cop I've met."

After another cup of coffee she suggested it might be better for her reputation if I trotted along.

"A widow, even one who'd broken up with her husband before he passed on, is expected to go through proper motions for the benefit of the townsfolk and their sensibilities."

"How long does that have to go on?"

"I'm not sure. With what I know now, it might not be more than a week. Maybe tomorrow. Why don't you drop around and check?"

I said I would.

13

A GREEN CHEVY, clean and polished, stood in front of Aunt Leck's and I made out two heads inside, a man and a woman. I halted at the sidewalk leading to the house and faced the car.

The man at the wheel opened his door, got out, and moved around the hood.

"Hear you've been looking for me," said Wes Fox.

"You got it wrong. I was looking for your girlfriend."

She came out the near door as Fox moved toward her, keeping his eye on me. It took a second for him to unlimber a grin.

"What do you want from her?"

"I'd like to know if she heard any talk between Lou and Yvette Hamsun when they sat together in the café those four Sundays just before he was killed."

He turned his head her way.

"You want to talk with this joker?"

"Why not? Let's go sit on the porch."

Aunt Leck's porch spanned the housefront, was a little deeper than most and sloped a tad down from the front door. The couple parked on a wicker settee and I took the rocker nearest Ella Parker.

I'd not had a clear view of her in the dance hall. In the dim light of the porch I got a strong impression of short blonde hair and a wide-cheeked face that seemed mostly mouth and eyes. She didn't wait for me to ask questions, just started in, talking like a woman telling secrets, low, solemn, and rushed.

"I didn't hear much of anything. She always shut up if I got close and so did he when he noticed me—except times he'd get so het up he wouldn't have paid me attention unless I dumped hot soup in his lap."

"Did she always come in at the same time?"

"Uh-huh. About five-thirty. She'd have her coffee by the time Lou showed up."

"What'd he talk about that you could catch?"

"That first night it was his kid, Mick. He was telling her how smart he was with the books and dumb everyway otherwise."

"How'd she react?"

"At first pretty standoffish. I mean you could tell it embarrassed her having him just move in and it didn't help any with him unloading about his son. She kept looking around like she was checking on who was watching all this. By the time I cleared the table and brought them dessert she was talking a little and not quite so, you know, nervous."

"You get the notion she thought Mick was anything special?"

"I guess maybe so. I mean, when he started talking Mick she paid more and more attention to him and sort of forgot about the impression they might be making. . . ."

"How about the later Sundays? She start to talk more?"

"Well, the second one I got the notion she was trying to tell him he shouldn't be eating with her, him being married and all. At first she was like the time before, looking around at other people in the dining room. But he seemed to sort of get through as the meal went on and again she wound up talking to him. Like I said, it was hard to hear much. She talked real low and always quit if she caught me so much as glancing their way. It really peeved me the way she acted like I might be trying to hear. I mean, a waitress is supposed to watch and see if customers want more coffee or need water or anything. . . ."

"Did you think he was trying to come on to her?" I asked.

"Oh, sure. He started it real sneaky but it was plain the last time. I think she was just playing hard to get. You look at her close and you know blamed well she's no cold fish like she pretends."

"What's the giveaway?"

"Well, it's in her eyes and the way she dresses and walks so proud. She can't kid me."

"You ever see any other guys try to move in?"

"Oh, sure. Colby Link, my boss, and the mayor. Others try to give her the eye but haven't got nerve enough to make any moves."

"What kind of moves did the mayor make?"

"Well, he happened by on Sundays, before Lou moved in. Not regular, like Lou, and he never tried to sit down and just move in but he'd manage to ask her about school, the library, and her work on the weekly paper. Tried to make it sound like he was the big politician worried about the townsfolk."

"And Colby?"

"He put up the new bookshelves in the library the first summer she was working there and they got chummy. I hear he hung around the library a lot. They say he's a great reader but I don't think he was before Yvette showed up. She's nice to him because it makes people think she's good-hearted and nobody's gonna think he's getting anywhere."

"She just feels sorry for him," said Fox.

"Oh, sure," said Ella, "just like she feels sorry for you and the other boys she taught. Especially the ones gaga over her."

"I was never gaga over her—"

"Oh, no, you just always talked about her until I wised you up to the fact she had you calf-eyed."

"Don't let the way she talks make you think she might be just a little jealous," Fox told me. "Like she keeps telling me, Ella hasn't got a jealous bone in her head."

"I don't," she said loftily. "I just get sick of boys mooning over a teacher who's no better than anybody else just because she's younger than all the other teachers and dresses up like she thinks she's a princess or something."

"Well, you're the only girl who took her class and didn't think she was special."

"I thought she was fine, I just didn't get all starry-eyed because I could see she was out to charm everybody silly just to make herself feel important."

"Ella's a great authority on human character," Fox told me. "She knows all about it because she's such a character herself."

Ella suddenly giggled. "Well, at least you've got one thing straight."

"How'd Albertson come on to her?" I asked.

"Oh, that didn't amount to anything, actually. He just always made a big thing of asking her how she liked the meal and stuff like that. He did that with nearly everybody but it was a little stronger with her. She sort of brings that out in all men."

She glared at Wes when she said that.

As I was deciding not to ask him how Yvette acted when they had their two dates, Ella leaned toward me and said, "Aren't you going to ask how she was when they went out together?"

"You think he'd tell me in front of you?"

"He probably wouldn't tell the truth. He tells me she was a perfect lady—that means she wouldn't let him smooch her."

"She treated me like a prize pupil," he said solemnly. "A model boy. It was almost like dating your own mother."

"Hah!" said Ella.

"Ella's insanely jealous. Won't believe me when I say I just went out with Yvette for educational purposes since I didn't learn all I needed to know in classes—"

She punched his shoulder and he shrank away, pretending pain. "See what I mean? Goes berserk. I'm all bruises—"

"She told him he should be planning a useful life," said Ella. "Setting goals and making plans. What she was doing was keeping him in his place only he's too simple to catch on."

"You've got it all wrong. Of course she knew I was too young and inexperienced for her, but recognized the promise and figured to help me realize it. That's why I became a plumber's helper. She made me see our future is in our country's sewer system and I should move up and be with the leaders."

"Oh, God," said Ella.

14

MONDAY MORNING I sat across the table from Yvette at Aunt Leck's boardinghouse and watched her while remembering Ella's evaluation and Wes Fox's fascination. Of course I was also going over the swimming hole party and the different woman she had been then. Nothing in her eyes or manner at the breakfast table gave a hint of what she'd shown making love. It had probably been damned dumb to get involved but there was no point in worrying that notion, since being cagey about women has never been my strong suit.

The library wasn't officially open on Mondays but Yvette told me she liked to go and putter even on days off so she walked with me to City Hall and asked what I'd been up to Sunday evening. I answered without detailing Ella's remarks and at the windup asked what she thought of the girl. She said Ella wasn't exactly an ideal student but was very perceptive and quick in relations with classmates and teachers.

"I'd call her people smart. She knows perfectly well Wes Fox doesn't want to get married, but she does, so she's put the word around that they're engaged, which very effectively traps him because he's the sort of fellow who'd never call a girl a liar.

His announcement to me at the dance won't change anything. I suppose it might have if I'd given him an ounce of encouragement, and in a way I feel guilty about not doing it. But she'll probably make a good wife and keep him out of trouble. She's not the sort he'll be able to cheat on and get away with it."

We parted at the stairway to the library and I went into my office and sat thinking things over. Mostly what I thought was I hoped it was a hell of a hot day and I could get Yvette swimming that night.

Dahlberg called a little before noon.

"This Wes Fox guy hasn't been in any trouble," he said. "All I got is he works for Bloom Plumbing as an apprentice. Old man Bloom's straitlaced as an Episcopal minister, so according to the cop who knows him, he wouldn't keep a guy he didn't think was anything but foursquare."

"Does this cop know the plumber well enough to maybe find out if Wes has any close friends, even a girlfriend in town there?"

"I thought of that. He says old Bloom wouldn't ask anything personal of anybody working for him. It's not like a family shop, you know? No kidding around, gossip, or feuds. On the job they talk about work and that's it."

I thanked him, hung up, and wished to hell I was working like in Greenhill where I was just the sidekick and could wheel over to Aberdeen and do my own checking while the real town cop kept the place in order and nobody missed me.

Yvette had left the library when I went up to check so I headed for Nordstrom's Café. Doris was busy behind the counter and didn't notice me until I'd reached the kitchen door and started through.

"Hey!" she yelled. "You can't go in there—"

"Too late," I said, and proved it.

The kitchen was tiny compared to what we had at the Wilcox Hotel in Corden. I could take in the whole room at a glance and sighted what had to be Nordstrom in a spotted white apron, sitting at a table against the wall, drinking coffee from a thick mug in his left hand while he scribbled on a tablet with his right.

I could see why he stayed out of sight of his customers. He wore a full beard, which in those days was about as common in South Dakota as tuxedos, his clothes were strictly from the trash can, and he peered at me with bloodshot eyes half hidden under eyebrows bushy as a Keystone Cop's mustache. He wasn't a sight to encourage large appetites.

For a second we stared at each other, then he took a swig from the heavy mug, put it down gently, and tilted his head toward the chair on the opposite side of the table.

I sat. Doris came in the door, bristling. Nordstrom told her to give me a cup of coffee in a voice gentle as a parson talking to a bereaved widow. She glared at me a second before pouring a cup that matched his, and brought it over. I helped myself to sugar and cream sitting on the table and stirred the brew. Doris went back out front.

I asked what he was writing and he said the day's menu.

"How long you been in Mustard?" I asked.

"Some eighteen years. Had this place six. Born, I'm told, on a farm near Sisseton. Raised by a squaw who cared for me till she died and I got passed around some before winding up here. Anything else you want to know?"

I leaned against the wall, staring at his hands. They seemed about the size of grizzly paws. "How'd you like Lou Dupree?"

"Six feet under, I like him fine."

"Was he messing with your wife?"

"Ask her."

"But did you think he was, that's the point I'm getting at."

He watched me soberly, not offended, just thoughtful.

"How many killers you put in jail?"

"Not many."

"I can believe it, seeing how you go at it. Did I have reason to kill Dupree? Some men might think so. Did I? No. He wasn't worth killing. He liked to think so. He was looking for somebody to do the job most his life."

I asked if it was okay to smoke in his kitchen and he said sure. I rolled one, lit up, and eased the smoke out while he watched patiently. Then he jerked his chin a notch and asked, "Why you roll your own?"

"It's cheap, takes a little talent to do it right, and gives me some satisfaction."

His sudden smile made him seem younger. His teeth were neatly separated and small, as if he'd never lost the first ones, only worn them down.

"You like being different, don't you? Kind of work at it."

"It's no work at all."

"You more'n likely won't ever find out who killed our cop. Too many people hated him. The only reason you got hired to make the try was the way he got it. Too messy, too deliberate. That kind of violence scares people. If he'd just been shot, nice and neat, or somebody slit his throat with a single slash, it'd all been accepted. But it was overdone. People in a town like Mustard can't handle excess."

"You use the library?" I asked.

The heavy eyebrows lifted a fraction.

"What makes you think that?"

"You sound like a man who's read some."

"I think a little. Watch folks."

"How much can you see from your kitchen?"

He smiled. I wondered if he had ever laughed.

"I wasn't born in it. I've seen a good deal. Don't feel any need to wander out there."

"So you kind of work at being different too, right?"

"You mean the beard and hunkering down here? I don't shave because my face can't tolerate a razor. Gives me rash. I'm not hiding, I just don't need all of it out there."

"What do you think of the mayor?"

"He's a politician."

"You don't like them?"

"What's to like? He's no better, no worse than most. He divides his business even between my place and Albertson's. His business is compromise, accommodation, and smoke screens. I accept all that, it's the way things are."

"What if Doris left you?"

"Ah," he said. "That's what strangers'd wonder. I didn't worry. Lou made her feel young a little. I didn't grudge that. But"—he smiled as angelically as his beard and eyes would allow—"it did simplify things when Dupree got killed. I didn't mourn. Wasn't even bothered by it being overdone. Matter of fact, it was, actually, damned satisfying."

Before leaving the café kitchen I learned Nordstrom's first name was Miles and he and his wife Doris had spent the evening hours of the murder night at home together. Neither pretended surprise that I asked, or showed any concern about giving their answers.

15

COLBY LINK MET me at the door as I left Nordstrom's Café and told me accusingly he'd been looking all over for me.

"Well, that's a tall task in a town Mustard's size. So what's the problem?"

"Mayor Tollefson wants you in his office, pronto."

When I headed that way Colby limped along sharply at my side as if I were under escort.

"What's the matter," I asked, "are the voters starting to lean on him?"

"The matter is, Mayor Tollefson wants every problem settled now, if not yesterday. He's never figured patience was a virtue."

"You get any notion he was worried that Monday morning he sent you to look up Lou Dupree?"

"Worried? No, he was more like annoyed. Always suspicioned Lou goofed off too much."

When we reached the mayor's office, Colby stopped in the doorway, announced that he'd found me, and limped off.

"Well," said the mayor when I was parked in a chair in front of his desk, "what's happening?"

"So far I'd say there are too many possibilities and not enough likelies."

He nodded as if that were precisely what he expected and suggested I list them in order.

"I'd start with any man in town who had a halfway attractive wife or girlfriend, add some of the livelier wives and girlfriends, throw in a few plain acquaintances, and even add a stranger or two."

"You're being facetious."

"Glad to hear it, I'd hate to make murder sound grim."

He decided that line didn't suit him any and switched directions as he leaned back in his chair.

"I know you're a character, but don't work it too hard. And I want to warn you against being cute with important people in town. Never offend people unnecessarily."

"Who's offended?"

"Doc Pelham tells me you questioned him about his wife's relations with Lou. You can't have been serious about that."

"I wasn't till now. When'd he complain?"

"It wasn't a complaint, he just remarked on it. You have to realize he's been embarrassed by his wife's flighty ways more than once so he's sensitive. Don't goad him. Particularly since Fran's about the last woman Lou'd try for."

"I don't know, seen some pretty unlikely couplings in my time. Never know what'll spark the flame."

"I think you'd find more fruitful territory with Miss Hamsun and that Fox fellow."

"You think they chopped him up between them?"

"I hope you're not being condescending. You admit you have no strong suspects and I'm only trying to stimulate thought. Earlier I told you I didn't want to influence your judgments of our people. I think you might try to appreciate my legitimate remarks and concern."

"Point made, Mr. Mayor. I've worked on the Fox angle most

of any so far because I had the same feeling you seem to. He's
one guy we know has a motive. He's also got the big head and
in spite of his business with Ella it's plain he's hot for Yvette
and probably resented the hell out of Lou trying to move on his
favorite schoolteacher. My problem is, he has a hell of a sense
of humor and that doesn't fit any of the killers I've known so far.
And like everybody else, he's got an alibi for the night of the
murder. I suppose you and your missus were together at home
the Sunday night Lou died?"

"We were. If you like, I'll call her to say you'll be over to
question her about that. All right?"

I said fine. The fact he promptly called only surprised me a
little and when I went my way he nodded good-bye in a style
that suggested we'd never be pals.

Cornelia answered my knock with what Ma would call deliberate speed. That is, she took her sweet time. I didn't realize
as I faced her through the screen that I'd never seen her on her
feet before, and it put me off a touch to find her tall enough to
look me straight in the eye. Her expression was somewhere
between guarded and curious and she didn't invite me in until
after I reminded her that her husband said I was to talk with
her.

"Of course," she said with a faint flutter, "do come in."

A moment later we were in their familiar living room. She
had the shades drawn only halfway and the windows raised so
the wind blew in, billowing the curtains and keeping the room
fresh and comfortable.

She settled into the chair she'd occupied the night we met,
I took the one her husband had sat in and waited for her to ask
if I'd take coffee.

She didn't. She just sat and watched me expectantly. Her
face was smooth as a window dummy's, but the eyes were bright
and watchful. Her nose was narrow. When I reached for my
tobacco bag she said, "Please, don't smoke."

I shoved it back in my shirt pocket and asked if she ever let her hair down.

"You mean literally, or actually?"

"Either."

"I let it down when I wash it. What's that got to do with your investigation?"

"Not much. What, besides the church, brings you and your friends together?"

"Bridge."

"You play regular?"

She crossed her legs, taking care to show nothing above the ankles, and nodded. "Every Friday night."

"With who?"

"Doctor Pelham and his wife, the Springers, and Albertsons. Now and again others join us. A few years back, the Duprees were quite regular substitutes. Jackie's a smart player, so was Lou."

My surprise showed and she smiled tolerantly. "You thought we'd consider them beneath us?"

"A bit."

"Do you play bridge?" she asked.

"No. When's the last time they played with you?"

"Oh, at least two years back. They were never regulars. Inviting them was my idea. I thought we should be democratic. Ken Albertson was very pleased, he was a great fan of our high school's athletic program and loved to talk about when Lou played on the team. That didn't quite enchant Doctor Pelham or our banker and his wife."

"How'd Lou behave at the bridge meetings?"

"Very nicely. The ladies liked him. He was polite and knew how to win gracefully and was very complimentary. He never let on he was bothered when he lost but I think he was."

"Did he flirt with you?"

"Oh, yes, he flirted with all of us. It was his way. None of us took it seriously."

"But they were dropped, right? Was that before or after they started breaking up?"

"I'd say they'd been breaking up from the time Mick was born. But that had nothing to do with our dropping them. It was more because Doctor Pelham and Philip Springer got fed up and stayed home several weeks in a row. Tolly told me we had to do something about that and I did. I think Jackie was quite happy to quit. I've no idea how Lou felt but suspect he resented it. Doctor Pelham said he was hard-nosed and thin-skinned."

"What was going on here the night Lou died?" I asked.

"Well, we were home and spent quite a bit of time talking about Lou Dupree. Tolly told me he had to find a way to get Lou out as the town policeman. He didn't think he was reliable or responsible. He was too interested in women and too neglectful of his duties."

"What women?"

She laughed a little too easily. "Any and all. Tolly wasn't bothered about him messing with Doris Nordstrom but he thought it unseemly he was publicly chasing after the school-teacher and felt he was altogether too familiar with all of us. Including me."

"How'd you like Lou?"

"I wasn't having an affair with him, but it was fun to have a man show interest. In a town like Mustard, you find yourself rather stretching your mind for distractions sometimes. He was good-looking and there was something dangerous about him. But none of us would be stupid enough to actually get involved."

"You think any of your group encouraged him?"

"I'm not sure. Maybe unintentionally some did. I may have myself— who knows what it takes? With a man like Lou, you could only reject him convincingly with a club."

"Or an ax."

"Well, yes, but obviously that was something more than a rejection."

"You ever get the notion Lou was interested in the doc's wife?"

"I told you, he flirted with us all. It meant nothing."

"I don't think Doc Pelham felt that way."

She met my stare directly and suddenly smiled.

"No. Dr. Pelham isn't casual about anything. I'd say he is a very intense man."

I thanked her and left.

16

THE VISIT WITH Mrs. Tollefson started me thinking about who had been the first woman Lou fooled with that his wife Jackie learned about. A little before noon I gave Jackie a call and she right off invited me over for lunch.

"You think the grace period's past?" I asked.

"I'm making it official," she answered.

She was wearing a simple dark gray housedress with white trim as she let me in. It fit her fine and she caught me admiring the view as I asked where Mick was. She said he'd gone to Aberdeen with Wes Fox the night before and led me into the kitchen. From the hip movements I was sure she wasn't wearing a girdle and on her that looked good.

"He's hoping to find a job that pays better than anything he can get here," she said as she started fixing lunch.

"He figured out how much it'll cost him when he's not getting free room and board?"

"Oh, yeah. But Wes said he can stay with him awhile."

"They old friends?"

"In a way. Wes was a year ahead of Mick and they shared no classes or friends. I've already told you Mick was never one for the ladies and of course Wes isn't one for much of anything else—but somehow they got together back when Mick was trying to promote his delivery service idea. Wes helped him start it—talking up merchants. Wes realized early it wasn't going to work and dropped out but they stayed friends."

She served ham-on-rye sandwiches, iced tea, and potato salad at the kitchen table.

"How'd Lou feel about Mick working with Wes Fox?" I asked as we started eating.

"Just what you'd expect—said Mick would come out short. They had a couple hot arguments about that but I finally squelched them. Of course Lou crowed when Wes dropped out."

"When did Lou first start messing with other women?"

She worked over a fresh bite of sandwich before answering.

"I was suspicious early on, but wasn't sure till about six years ago."

"Who were you sure about?"

She sipped iced tea and studied me awhile before answering.

"I don't think that's got anything to do with what happened a week ago. Why do you ask?"

"That was back when you and Lou were still playing bridge with the Tollefsons, Pelhams, and all, right?"

She sighed. "I guess you've been talking with Cornelia. She never has liked Fran Pelham."

"I got the notion she didn't mind letting me know that. What tipped you off?"

"Things like a smudge of lipstick on Lou's hand after he and Fran had been alone a few minutes in the kitchen, and her going up to the bathroom right after they came out, like she was going to retouch her mouth. That and his smug expression. The week after, when we played at the Tollefsons', Doc got a call to deliver a baby at a farm west of town and almost as soon as we got home and into bed there was a call and Lou went downstairs to answer it. He came back and said it was a man named Clinger who was all frantic about someone stealing his cow and he had to charge off and check it out. He was gone over two hours and in the morning told me, very casually, it'd been a false alarm."

"Somebody told me he was a real churchy guy," I said.

"Being holy never stopped any man from philandering that I've ever known. I think they're the worst. What made me madder than anything else was him acting like I should be fool enough to accept that stupid story, close my eyes, and pretend everything was dandy. That was the morning I told him he'd never have me again."

"He get mad?"

"Roaring. Said I was a frigid bitch and anything that happened from then on was my fault. Later he tried to get lovey but I never let him touch me again. Four months ago he finally moved out. I think that's the best thing ever happened to me. I only wish I'd raised enough hell when I first caught on to drive him out six years back."

She sipped iced tea and stared past me a moment, then met my eyes and grinned. "So," she said, "you think Doc Pelham got carried away with an ax?"

"It hardly seems the tool for a doctor, but on the other hand, maybe he figured that's what everybody'd think. And just maybe, the ax, or a hatchet, was all that'd give him the satisfaction he needed."

"Doc's very intense. It's not hard to picture him going after Lou. You talked with Fran yet?"

"Guess I'll have to."

"Why the hesitation?"

"The mayor's sort of warned me off. Doesn't want Doc Pelham upset."

"Well, I'll just invite Fran over here for a chat. Then you can blame me."

"Will she come?"

"You bet. Fran and I had an understanding way back—when Lou quit visiting her. She came and made a confession. It did her a world of good. I'll call her."

I drank more iced tea while she was gone and marveled at women.

It took Fran Pelham just fifteen minutes to arrive. Like Jackie, she wore a housedress, only hers was ruffly and trimmed with blue flowers nobody ever saw in a garden or wood. The plump body was girdled and squeezed into her dress, the blondish hair was fluffy as a cotton ball, her eyes had the blue innocence of a perfect summer sky, and her mouth hardly looked wide enough to admit double straws.

She batted her eyes slowly, the way a butterfly opens and closes its wings while resting on a blossom.

She joined us at the table, accepted iced tea, added two spoonfuls of sugar, and stirred it gently, making the ice spin and ring on the glass sides. She acknowledged Jackie's introduction of me with a blush and smile that made the tiny mouth widen to expose prominent white teeth.

"We were talking about Lou," Jackie explained, "and I told Carl you knew him pretty well and might be able to help him in his investigation."

"I don't see how anything I know would help," she said with a flutter of hands.

"Don't be embarrassed," said Jackie, "I've told Carl everything and he understands. In his work he learns all about people. He doesn't think ill of you at all—we know whatever happened was Lou's fault. Who'd he start seeing after he broke off with you?"

It took quite a while but eventually she said she believed it had been Cornelia.

"I mean, I just don't know who else it could've been, except that woman at the café he'd been involved with forever. He was with her before me, you know."

It was plain that was something Jackie didn't want covered and it tickled me to find she had a snobbish streak.

"What made you think he got in with Cornelia?"

"Well, he always had eyes for her, you know, and would've taken a very special satisfaction out of her being the mayor's wife. I'm sure the only reason he seduced me was to get at The Doctor."

I found she always referred to her husband as The Doctor. You could hear the capitals in her tone.

"You mean he wanted to seduce her and you because he hated Tolly and your husband for getting him dumped from the bridge club?"

"Of course. He was always telling me what snobs they were and how they hated him because he was more appealing to women than they were. He was really pitiful sometimes. So obsessed!"

"Did your husband know anything for sure about you and Lou?" I asked.

Up until then I'd had brains enough to leave the questioning to Jackie and right away found I should've kept my mouth shut. She suddenly looked frightened.

"No, of course not. He never suspected a thing." She pushed her glass away and got to her feet.

"I really should get home. I promised The Doctor we'd have ham loaf tonight and I have to go to the butcher for the meat and mix it up and all. It's been very nice meeting you, Mr. Carl, thank you for the iced tea, Jackie, good-bye."

When she was gone I looked at Jackie.

"He knew, didn't he?" I said.

"You can bet on it. Doc Pelham has always known what was going on around him, believe me."

17

THE MAYOR TOLD me that Lou Dupree's pastor was named Per Skogslund and he lived in a big white house on the far side of the Methodist church three blocks from Main Street going south on Third Avenue.

I saw the old man sitting on his porch nodding over a heavy book as I approached under the shade of elms lining the street. He didn't glance up until I stopped at the bottom step and greeted him by name.

His pale blue eyes recognized me at once, he smiled, put the book on the floor, rose, and offered his hand.

"Officer Wilcox—to what do I owe this honor?"

Being addressed as "officer" was enough to rattle me but his suggesting my visit was an honor just about made me tongue-tied. I managed to keep from saying aw shucks, took his hand, and said I needed a little help.

"Anything at all," he said, "I'd be delighted! Care for iced tea, or perhaps some lemonade?"

"Don't bother—"

"No bother—Signa'd be delighted. Here, sit down—I'll just tell her what you'd like—"

I accepted iced tea and it was delivered with ceremony by his hefty, gray-haired, beaming wife who also provided sugar, a long spoon, and goodwill. The pastor got a glass of lemonade.

When Signa had gone back inside and we were settled down he asked again what he could do for me.

"I guess you know what my main job is here?" I said.

"Of course, to replace our unfortunate Lou. A highly responsible role—"

"It's simpler than that. I'm supposed to find who killed him. Everything else is going through the motions."

"Ah," he said, nodding. "So what do you expect from me?"

"You said Lou was a regular at your church. Did you get to know him personally enough to tell me anything about him?"

A shadow passed over the battered face.

"I doubt," he said, "that anyone ever knew Lou in a personal way. I saw him in church every Sunday, but except for two or three occasions we never talked seriously."

He took a couple swallows of lemonade, put the glass down, folded his hands, and slouched back in his wicker chair.

"You know he was in combat in France during the World War?"

I nodded.

"Saw a great deal of action. All the horrors of mass slaughter. Had no illusions about glories of war—he lost all of his friends and turned to Jesus, you might say, under high duress. I think he almost resented his need for the church and he had the devil's own contrary spirit. I'm sure you're well aware by now that he had an uncontrollable hunger for women?"

"That's what I've heard."

"Yes. Obsessive. And the town became obsessed with his weakness. He was, I think, quite an intelligent man. He could never have gotten away with his philandering and woman chasing if he hadn't been so clever, although sometimes I suspect persistence gets satyrs further with woman catching than charm, wit, or brilliance."

"His approach to the schoolteacher was cute," I said.

"How so?"

"He got to her through her interest in his son. Tried to make her think his real aim was to get her help in making things right between Lou and the kid. For a while it worked—at least she ate meals with him."

"Yes. His other technique was in convincing women their husbands didn't appreciate them. He was most successful at that."

"Nordstrom thinks he worked at getting himself killed."

"Ah," nodded the pastor, "Miles Nordstrom is no fool, however odd he may appear. The truth, I suspect, is that Lou Dupree hated himself. He was a driven man. What a waste! I think he felt guilty that he didn't die in Flanders Field with his comrades."

"How well do you know Doc Pelham?"

"Only professionally. He has tended my wife on a few occasions and of course we've met a few times at community affairs. Seems a most competent physician although a trifle aloof. He does not attend any church."

"How about Fran, his wife?"

"She's a Lutheran. Or so I hear. I doubt that she's deeply involved in anything spiritual."

"You hear she had an affair with Lou?"

"I don't encourage that sort of gossip, Officer Wilcox. But I won't deny I heard of it." He was silent for a moment and then darted me a sharp look. "Really—you aren't suggesting—?"

"I have to check all the possibilities."

"No," he shook his head. "Doctor Pelham couldn't have done it."

"Who could?"

He frowned, shook his head, then smiled sympathetically.

"All right, I see your point. Of course no one in town can

accept the notion any one of us could do such a thing. Yet, it had to be one of us."

"But so far, everybody's got an alibi."

He chuckled. "All right, you've got me. I have no alibi whatsoever. I took a walk Sunday evening. Frequently do that after evening services. It is a particularly good moment for me. I've been a pastor for over twenty years and I still get nervous in front of my congregation. Can you imagine that? No, I suspect you can't. You aren't a man who takes himself seriously, who fears people will see through him or anticipates making a fatal blunder. I am, and I do. So Sunday night the pressure eases and I feel free and at peace. I walk and look at the sky and thank God for all he's given me, my wife, my work, and the people who, perhaps foolishly, look up to me. Well, not all of them by any means. I'm sure the mayor looks down a good way before he finds Pastor Skogslund. But he comes to my church and he supports it loyally and generously. But I ramble—a notoriously common fault with my kind—so I admit to you, I cannot account for my whereabouts that fatal eve. I remember seeing no one—I didn't wish to—"

"Did Lou ever show any interest in your wife?"

For a second he stared and then he laughed so hard he bent over. After a few seconds he subsided and leaned back once more.

"No, I can't recall that Lou ever showed any interest in Signa beyond her chocolate pie. You would have a great problem in finding a motive for me. Although I'll admit, life will probably be simpler with no Lou to upset my congregation with his bad example and his impact on family serenity in general. I doubt you could weave a firm case from that."

"Sometimes," I said, "a cop has to be pretty creative."

"Well, lots of luck, Officer Wilcox."

"Just call me Carl."

"Very well, thank you. Mind if I ask a question?"

"Shoot."

"Your church attendance Sunday, was that because of Yvette, or did you only come to observe the congregation?"

"About half and half."

"I guessed as much. Yvette is a very lonely woman. I hope you won't be offended if I urge you not to take advantage of her."

"You think Lou did?"

"I was never certain of anything but that he would try."

"How about Wes Fox?"

He frowned. "No, I don't think that likely. Much too young for her. But the fact that she encouraged him even slightly seemed out of character to me. Except for that, she has been totally discreet."

He thought for a moment, then gave me a sudden piercing glance. "I was surprised to hear she went to the dance with you Saturday night too. Evidently I don't really know her at all. How did you manage that?"

I told him.

He smiled sadly. "So, your style is not altogether unlike Lou's, is it?"

"As the ladies always say, Pastor, us men are all alike."

18

AUNT LECK SERVED a tuna hot dish for supper, which tasted better than it smelled but not much. I got questions from some of the oldtimers at the table about how the investigation was going and my answers didn't impress anybody, including me. Yvette kept quiet through it all.

On the way out of the dining room I invited her to walk with me and she agreed casually, which, considering our recent coziness, seemed a little weird. I got the picture quick when she asked after our first few steps how I got along with the new widow at lunch.

"If you know I lunched with her, I suppose you also know that Fran Pelham came around to join us?"

"Yes. Later."

"You spy with your own glasses or do you use agents?"

"Mustard is a goldfish bowl. Everybody watches. I know you met with Pastor Skogslund, too."

"But that doesn't bother you, right?"

"I don't consider him a threat. Jackie's something else."

"She is. She's also the one who should know the most about Lou so I'll probably huddle with her again before this thing's squared away. You figure you ought to come along with me whenever I talk to a woman?"

"Not really." She suddenly grinned a little and cocked her head at me. "I just happen to have heard a lot about you. Aunt Leck has been gathering information, all for my own good, you understand. What did Pastor Skogslund say about me?"

"He said he hoped I wouldn't take advantage of you."

"How sweet. Did you make any promises?"

"None."

"I suppose he was surprised I went to the dance with you."

"He sounded more surprised that you dated Wes Fox twice. He thought that was out of character."

"Which just goes to show he doesn't know anything about me."

"He's about decided he doesn't."

She laughed and said he was actually a very nice man, probably about the only honest one she knew. I wondered if she'd consider me honest if I suggested we take another swim, but put off the question. We walked awhile in silence and finally I asked what she was thinking.

"I'm thinking that if you decide to buy any rubbers, please don't do it in Mustard."

"Your supply out?"

"They come in packages of three so I still have two."

I decided against saying that sounded promising because it was plain this woman wouldn't accept anything being taken for granted.

We walked a little further without any gab and upon reaching the end of the street with nothing beyond but prairie, she stopped and faced me.

"Have you ever been serious about any woman?"

"I've been downright grim more than once. Even been married."

"Really? I hadn't heard that. What happened? Where'd you meet her?"

"New York, after the war. She was playing a French horn in a band at a concert somebody gave me a free ticket to. I got a smile from her during the show and hung around the stage door and met her coming out. We married two weeks later, I brought her back to South Dakota, she didn't like it and went back. For some reason she didn't think Corden stacked up too good against New York."

"So you're divorced."

"Yup. Desertion. Because I wouldn't go back with her. No alimony, no kids, no regrets. I got my money's worth out of the whole business just watching Ma's face the first time I brought Babe into the hotel in Corden."

She stared at me, shook her head, and started walking back toward town.

"It sounds like an elaborate practical joke."

"Yeah. It's the last I ever pulled."

"And now you paint signs and solve murders."

"I'm a better sign painter than a detective. In the first case I always know what I'm doing, in the second I never do."

"I guess you won't be in Mustard long, will you?"

"Not likely. Just like you."

"Not just like. It isn't so easy for a woman to be footloose. I'll admit it's what I'd like. Somehow I've got to find a way to get out from under this business of living under rules dictated by Victorian busybodies. Dating Wes was nothing more than a small show of defiance. Frankly I was disappointed it didn't cause more of a stir. Tolerating Lou was more of the same and more exciting but when I realized what a self-centered, destructive nit he was, I put a stop to it. Would you like to buy me an ice cream soda?"

I would and did and we sat in a corner of the soda fountain run by a stout middle-aged character who sat behind the spigots and counter, reading a *Liberty* magazine between servings to mostly youngsters.

"Tell me about you," said Yvette, making the most appealing pitch women know and so of course I blabbed. A lot of it was true and I stuck in laughs where it might sound like bragging or even apologizing and she lapped it up while inhaling her soda.

I told of cowboying, rustling, soldiering, and life as a hobo, a convict, and growing up in a hotel run by puritanical parents and having a sister who was the town belle and joy of life for Ma and Pa.

Walking back to Aunt Leck's I tried to promote a return to the swimming hole and all that went with that but she wouldn't go for it. She did agree to a walk beyond the livelier part of town and allowed some pretty heavy smooching but that's as far as I could get and after returning her to the boardinghouse, went about my duties as the night watchman feeling fired up enough to climb the water tower and see how far I could jump.

19

PETTY CRIME AND going against the moral grain pay poor dividends in a small town. When you grow up where all the faces are familiar, a boy who steals or a girl who's easy both get identified early and are permanently marked. They don't have to be branded or wear scarlet letters for instant character identification by the natives. Of course even in small towns the upper classes have advantages. If you're the son of a man with money and position, you can raise hell and only get called high-spirited. His daughter will be considered independent if she pets too easy and may be called wild if she goes all the way. Poor boys in trouble are called sneaky at best and thieves at worst. Poor girls are tramps if they pet with poor boys and strumpets if they take on guys better off.

Fred Hicks was marked from birth since his mother, Riva Sutter, was known as a loose woman even before she got pregnant by Eli Hicks, who was a well-known drunk, sneak thief, and the type of man who'd seduce a retarded girl.

Fred got through high school with the lowest average grade level of any kid in Mustard but was allowed to graduate, according to Colby Link, because he was the fastest runner in the county and the school's athletic coach managed to coax, bully, and argue teachers into letting him stay in school through his four years so he could be on the track team and play football.

"He wasn't any great shakes as a blocker," Colby said, "but he was always so scared and fast he was hell to catch as a ball carrier if you could shake him loose around end. Into the line? Forget it."

That summer he was working at the icehouse, cutting and delivering ice to homes in town.

I drifted over to where Hicks worked directly from Aunt Leck's in the late morning and found him wearing a heavy leather apron with leg protectors and loading the ice wagon. His long face was ruddy, the eyes close-set, deep brown, and wary. He had a short nose and a long chin and had worked up a good sweat. He welcomed a break and offered me a cigarette when he dug a pack from his shirt pocket. I took it, to be sociable, and lit us both up.

"Well," he said, "what you want first? Where was I the night the cop got killed, or how much do I know about old Lou?"

"Take your pick."

He grinned like a hungry crocodile, closed to take a puff on the cigarette, and glanced toward the horse hitched to his wagon.

"Well, like you probably know, I played football with old Lou. He wasn't anything special at it—basketball's where he shined. Heard him say more'n once it was twice the fun hitting guys who weren't padded. We were never buddies."

"You know how early on he got close to Jackie?"

He glanced at me and looked back toward the horse, which was twitching its tail at flies on its flank.

"I didn't pay that much attention. They were steady their senior year, that's all I know for sure."

"Where were you that Sunday night?"

"No place special. Had dinner at Nordstrom's, walked around a little, went to bed early."

"Where you live?"

"I got a room at Agatha Jones's house."

"Lou ever give you any trouble?"

"Why'd he give me trouble?"

"I kind of got the impression he gave just about everybody some of that. Wouldn't think he'd have neglected you."

"Well, some blabbermouth'll probably tell you so I might's well. We had a fight in school once. When we were seniors. He thought I was trying to move in on Jackie."

"Weren't you?"

"Well, hell yes, but I mean it wasn't going any place. He was bigger and better looking, family wasn't poor like mine, I couldn't have got anywhere and he knew it. It was plain meanness.

"He punched you out?"

"Well, it wasn't like he beat me to any pulp—I wasn't dumb enough to try and take him, but he belted me with a sneak punch that about broke my head and jumped me when I went down. I managed to cover enough to keep from getting broken up but it all happened in front of a crowd and it wasn't any fun, I'll tell you."

"You kind of went for Jackie, huh?"

"About half the class did, sure. She was cuter than hell and a barrel of fun and never a snob. Treated me real nice."

"You ever marry?"

"Uh-huh. She run off with a drummer who used to stay at Bert's hotel regular. Mae, my wife, was working for Bert, making beds, doing the wash and all that stuff. It was no big loss."

"Lou ever try to make her?"

"Probably. He tried to get in every woman's pants in town."

"But you don't know if he managed with your wife?"

"Well, if he had, you think I'd waited six years to get even with him?"

"Somebody got more than even. And maybe you just never had a good chance before last week."

"You're crazy. If I'd killed the son of a bitch I'd been bragging it up all over town. I'm just ashamed I didn't do it and I'd be the first to pin a medal on whoever did so make whatever the hell you want of that."

He finished his cigarette, squashed it with his shoe, picked up the ice tongs, and said he had to get back to work.

"You know the schoolteacher, Yvette?" I asked.

"Why wouldn't I? She's been in town two years now, you can't miss her."

"You know Lou was trying to work on her?"

"Course I did, what the hell, I may be dumb but I'm not deaf or blind. So what?"

"Thought maybe you might be sweet on her."

"Well, I'm not dead either, but I sure as hell wasn't giving old Lou any competition. Besides, he wasn't getting anywhere with her."

"How'd you know that?"

"Well, she cut him dead that last Sunday, didn't she?"

"In a way, I guess so."

"So all right. I'll see you around, I suppose."

He climbed up to the wagon seat, slapped the reins, and moved off.

20

AGATHA JONES'S WHITE house stood on a shallow lot mid-block just a ways from downtown. The grass was green without dandelions or plantain and looked freshly mowed. A neat white outhouse stood in back under a big apple tree. Agatha was sitting on the front porch crocheting something white, and so far, small.

She watched me approach with a guileless smile only small old ladies and a few young kids can produce.

I said hi and introduced myself.

She said she was happy to meet me and sounded like she meant it. I guessed she was one of those people with a weakness for mongrels over thoroughbreds.

"Fred Hicks tells me he boards here," I said.

She glanced up without a hitch in the stitching and smiled. "You think he lies?"

"Just checking. That's what you do in my business."

"I suppose so." Her eyes went back to her handwork. "Well, he does."

"How long?"

"Be a year in September."

"Was he around a week ago Sunday night?"

"Oh, yes." She lowered the crocheting stuff into her lap and peered at me through thick lenses. "He was in and out all evening, which was typical. Mr. Hicks is a quiet but restless man. It's like he can't decide what to do with himself. I'd judge it's all because of his wife leaving him. It's like she took part of his soul with her and he's wanting to go find it but doesn't know where to start and isn't sure he wants it." She smiled slyly. "You think I'm a little touched?"

I sat on the porch floor and leaned against a post flanking the steps.

"No. You make sense. What else do you know about him?"

"He's a pitiable man. Never had a chance, what with his simple mother and good-for-nothing father. Some people'd be better off coming from something like a turtle so they'd never even see their parents. Total fresh start. Of course that'd only be good if everybody started the same. What're your parents like?"

"Puritans."

"Oh, dear." She actually looked dismayed.

"Did you know Lou Dupree?"

"Yes. And his mother and father too. Father was a judge, you know. Here in Mustard. Very distinguished man, not as tall as Lou, but with a handsomer nose and gray, neatly trimmed sideburns. They say he was a good judge but I wouldn't really know, since I was never in his court. Lou's mother, poor thing, was a mouse. Nobody remembers her."

"What happened to the judge?"

"Died young. Heart. Wife went back East where she had relatives. Lou was fresh married then to that lovely Schoop girl, Jackie. But it never worked out, you know. Everybody claims the war spoiled him. I don't believe it. He was a contrary child from the start and anybody could tell he wasn't normal from his reputation in school sports. Folks said he was the dirtiest player anybody ever knew. That made him a sports hero, if you can imagine. Then he went into service and they say he was a hero in war. He loved that. But back in Mustard with no games to play or Germans to kill, he was nothing. Lou Dupree figured everybody owed him love because he'd been a hero. It made him believe he was owed unqualified love and approval. That's what made him a hater, a hopeless husband, and a bad father."

"Who you think might've killed him?"

"About half the men in town, and maybe as many women."

"That bad?"

She laughed and shook her head.

"Don't you know when you're being kidded?"

"Not too sure. You have any reason to take an ax to him?"

"Well," she said thoughtfully, "I certainly got annoyed enough so I'd like to have poked him with one of my needles when he wouldn't arrest the Healy boy for stealing apples from my tree last fall, but that wasn't quite enough to make me commit murder with a hatchet. Except maybe on that Healy brat—who was still healthy the last I heard."

"Did you know Mae Hicks, Fred's wife that ran off?"

"Oh, yes. She lived in the house half a block west and across the street. Homely little mutt as a child, had a fine figure when she grew up. I suppose that was her downfall. Men chased her for only one reason and she made the most of it until she got pregnant. Married Fred because he was the only fellow willing to take credit, and, I suspect, it was the only way he ever got a chance to make love to her. She had a miscarriage right after the marriage—which was before a justice of the peace in Aberdeen. The marriage, I mean, not the miscarriage. People never stopped talking about that. I suspect the real reason Mae left Fred was that for all her foolishness, she was way too bright and spritely for a dull one like Fred."

"You hear Dupree was after her?"

"Of course."

"Was he messing with her over a long time?"

"Not so long—maybe a couple months. Lou never fooled around long with the easy ones."

"How long was it after he dropped Mae before she left town?"

"No more than a month or two."

"Where's she now?"

"Heard she was back in South Dakota. Aberdeen, I believe. When she left Mustard she and the Schwartz boy—the one she ran off with—went to California. She was gone nearly a year before coming back. Somebody told me she was waitressing in a restaurant downtown there."

"What happened to the Schwartz boy?"

"I heard he went to prison for car stealing. No surprise. He stole cars a couple times here in town when he was a kid. Somehow learned how to start them without keys."

I asked what last name Mae was using and she said she'd gone back to her maiden name, Olson. She talked some more but gave me nothing else useful and after thanks I went back downtown.

21

JUST AFTER PASSING Albertson's Café I heard Colby Link call and turned to find him standing by the door looking annoyed.

"The mayor wants you," he said, tilting his head toward the café.

I went back and followed him to the booth by the kitchen door where Tollefson sat, working on a hot pork sandwich. He waved me onto the bench across from him, nodded good-bye to Link, and took a swig of coffee before speaking.

"You have quite a way with the ladies," he said, making it plain he considered that talent a fault.

"Yeah? How come I can't keep one?"

He pushed his greasy plate forward a notch, wiped his mouth with a paper napkin, and frowned.

"I don't like you getting cute."

"Why don't you just tell me what's your beef?"

"You talked with Doctor Pelham's wife after I most specifically told you not do."

I leaned my elbows on the table between us and folded my hands under my chin.

"There's a few things wrong with that, Mr. Mayor. First, you weren't all that specific, second you don't know the circumstances, third I never made any promises, and finally I'm not your errand boy, I'm the town cop. Sworn to enforce the law and all that. There wasn't anything in the oath that said I had to love, honor, and obey the mayor."

He studied me all through that speech and stayed at it after I shut up. Then he nodded, glanced around the café, and leaned forward.

"Did you learn anything?"

"It's pretty plain his wife was messing with Lou."

He leaned back once more. "That doesn't mean Doc Pelham killed him."

"Right. But it gives him a dandy motive."

He met my eyes straight on, leaned his head against the booth back, and finally said, "A good many had the same motive."

"Uh-huh. Including you."

"I never believed Cornelia actually let him seduce her. I don't doubt she flirted with him in her quiet way—but that's all. And certainly, I'd never have made you the town officer if there'd been any reason for me to be concerned about the problem you suggest."

"Everybody's alibied," I agreed. "Except the preacher and Fred Hicks."

He actually smiled. "You have a motive for the preacher?"

"Not much. He didn't take the notion seriously that Lou made a try for his wife but he admitted his death ended a lot of problems for his parish."

The smile got thinner. "What about Fred?"

"His landlady says Lou had his wife about six years back. And she tells me Fred was in and out Sunday night and has been brooding. She thinks his wife took part of Fred's soul when she left."

"That sounds like Agatha. So now what?"

"I think I should make a trip to Aberdeen. Talk with Mae Olson. Oh, another thing—you know where Amelia is now?"

He considered his answer just a half second before answering, "I believe she's in Aberdeen."

"Got a shop?"

"I think so."

"Who'd you deputize when Lou took a day off?"

"Colby Link."

"Ah. How come you didn't promote him to town cop when Lou got killed?"

"I didn't think we wanted a crippled man handling the police job full-time."

"But he can do it in between, huh?"

"It's worked in the past."

"So it won't be any problem if I'm gone for a day."

"I suspect the town will survive."

"Okay, after I eat lunch I'm taking off. You want to tell Colby he's on duty?"

"I will."

I went back to Aunt Leck's for my car and told her I'd be gone overnight. She wanted to know where. I said it didn't matter to her and she argued she should know if folks were looking for the town cop. I told her to send all that crowd to Colby and left her sizzling.

I thought some of letting Yvette and Jackie know what I was up to but scratched it to avoid any chance of Wes Fox and Mick Dupree getting advance warning. My showing up unexpected might tip them a little off balance and I needed any advantage available.

22

MY OLD MAN moved back to South Dakota from Michigan because he loved open country where the land stretched out near flat and you never get surprised by the weather sneaking up from behind mountains, high hills, or even too many trees. Some folks think it's monotonous driving over such land but if you didn't have to go more than a hundred miles and kept a good watch, there were plenty of changes and lots of fine sights even back in the mid-thirties when the land was parched and the grain turned brown under the naked sun. The roads run straight, mostly, and over and over you see them narrow to a point on the horizon, and now and again, when you top a gentle rise, you sight it stretching even further. In the Depression days you'd not see a single car coming at you in all that eternal spread under the endless blue sky bowl but you'd often sight pheasants, gophers, or even a deer.

Aberdeen is flat as any town gets, has lots of tree-lined streets, and is the third largest town in South Dakota. That doesn't give the locals any bragging rights but still makes the more uppity citizens look down their noses at people from places like Corden and Mustard where folks can only look down on farmers.

I stopped at the police station and visited with Dahlberg, who wasn't one of the uppity types and had helped me in the past. He gave me Wes's address and looked up Amelia Parridine's shop in downtown but couldn't help with Mae Olson.

Amelia was with a customer when I called her number and couldn't be disturbed according to a snooty young thing who obviously figured men had no business calling. I told her to tell the boss I was a cop who wanted to ask questions.

That brought silence and when I said "Hello?" I got no response for several seconds. Then a husky voice said, "Yes?"

I told her my name and business and asked what time the shop closed.

"I'll be busy till six," she said. "What's this about?"

"Lou Dupree's murder."

"I know nothing about it."

"You haven't heard what happened?"

"Well, yes, of course, but I've not seen him in years and can't imagine why the police would want to talk to me."

"I'll tell you what, Mrs. Parradine, I'll buy you supper and we'll talk about it, okay?"

She thought about that for all of half a second and asked if I'd come around to the shop and pick her up at six-ten.

She wasn't quite as flashy as I'd expected from the Mustard citizens' descriptions, but she was still a woman you'd look at twice anywhere you met. The dress had no furbelows and fit her soon at the waist and maybe a touch early across the hips. She wore heels higher than most and enough jewelry to add weight without slowing her any. I guess she's the first woman I ever saw wearing phony eyelashes.

She was saying good-bye to her last customer by the door as I walked in the didn't even glance my way until the farewells were complete and the woman left. Then I got her full attention.

"Officer Wilcox?" she said with a faint note of disappointment.

"You thought I'd be taller."

She laughed and shook her head. "My God, am I so transparent?"

"You still willing to eat with me?"

"I'm not sure. Not because you aren't tall but because I don't know how well I can deal with a mind reader. Did you know I also expected you to have a pot?"

"No."

"All right, in that case I'll go quietly. Just give me a second to check with the mirror."

She was back in a couple seconds, ushered me out, locked the door, and asked if I'd picked a restaurant.

"You know the town better, you pick it."

"I think I could get to like you. Let's just stroll to the right here and there's a nice place near the corner."

"You born a blonde?" I asked.

"Of course. Unfortunately by the time I was nineteen it became dark and since that just wasn't me, I turned to the bottle. Bleach, that is. Am I a suspect in your case?"

"I don't know—how good are you with an ax or a hatchet?"

"I'm not sure—can't remember ever trying. Anyway, I have an alibi for that Sunday night."

"Good. Tell me about it."

"I can't. He's married."

We were entering the café when she handed me that and we didn't get back to the subject until we were seated in a booth with high backs and padded seats and had gone over the menu and ordered.

"Okay," I said, "you're messing with a married man. If it comes down to your neck or his, would you stick yours out?"

"No, but I don't think it'll come to that. You don't seriously think I made a special trip to that miserable town and chopped up Lou, do you?"

"No."

The waitress brought us coffee and we doctored it up and drank. Amelia held her cup with both hands while peering at me from under her awning eyelashes. Her eyes were such a deep blue I wondered if she'd found a way to paint them.

"You're not really a cop, are you?" she asked.

"I'm not an Aberdeen cop so I've no business questioning you about a murder in Mustard. But I have been hired to find out who did the job."

"You're like a private eye, really."

"If you like. How about you tell me what went on between you and Dupree, and what you learned about all the townspeople you got to know during your stay there."

"That could take us deep into the evening."

"I've got the time."

"And the inclination, I'll bet. Okay. I imagine you've already picked up the common gossip—Lou Dupree came on strong and turned nasty when I wasn't friendly. I'll have to admit, if I was ever going to kill anybody, Lou'd been my choice. The dumb thing is, the man wasn't unattractive. I mean, I could have been interested if he'd shown any sense. But he acted like I owed him a lay in the hay just because that's what he wanted. He said everything about me advertised availability and I had no business saying no. At first I thought it was funny, but it didn't take long to learn the man didn't own a sense of humor. When I told him to hit the road he was furious, tried to get me thrown out of the hotel—"

"Bert wouldn't go for it, right?"

"He was beautiful, that little, dried-up old man. I could've kissed him. As a matter of fact, when I left I did. It made his eyes water. He was a real sweetie."

"Did the mayor come on to you?"

"Not really. I could tell he'd like to but for all of his self-assurance and bluster, he's a little boy at heart and I scared him. I suppose some of the reason I overdo things is because I just plain like to push men off balance. The trouble is, I've never in my life been able to deal with other women. I have to work on men and they have all the power so I just take every advantage I can wangle and I've not done too badly."

"What about the banker?"

"Philip? Now there's a case. He'd love to have arranged things but didn't have the gall."

"He didn't proposition you?"

"A woman like me doesn't get propositioned unless she lets it happen. I never did. In a town that size, there's no way you can mess around and not have everybody knowing it. Hell, everybody knows it even if it doesn't happen—know what I mean?"

I nodded.

"Not that I was interested in him. He's not at all my kind of man even if he does have money. Actually I'm very fussy about men."

"But you don't care if they're married?"

The waitress brought our orders and I saw Amelia scowling thoughtfully as she organized her plate with the meat nearest her and the mashed potatoes a little beyond on the right.

After she'd tried everything she paused and gave me a dark frown.

"Somehow I didn't expect you'd be a judgmental person. That just shows it doesn't pay to make assumptions on looks "

"I wasn't passing judgment," I said. "Just trying to get the picture."

"The picture is, I'm just like everybody else except maybe more honest. I'm selfish. I don't go around being Miss Goody Two-shoes and worrying about whose toes get stepped on when I go after what I want. On the other hand I don't cheat people, or lie if I don't have to, or say snotty things that hurt. I think faster than most but don't take advantage of it real often. And I've no false modesty, in case you haven't noticed."

"Okay," I said, "I'm all disarmed. What'd you think of Colby Link?"

She concentrated a moment on her pork chop, carefully removing fat and cutting a dainty bite clear. When she'd chewed it and swallowed she met my eyes again.

"What do you think of him?" she asked.

"Haven't made up my mind. He seems to have a grudge but I'm not sure where it's aimed. He's the mayor's boy, it seems, all the way, but I don't think he likes him or anyone else who has two good legs."

"He liked me," she said with no false modesty.

"I can see why."

For the first time her smile was flirtatious.

I smiled back and asked her what Colby thought of Lou Dupree.

She suddenly turned sober and thoughtful.

"That's a good question. There was something strange between them. Very mixed. I think Colby was kind of caught between admiring the boy he'd shared growing up and playing basketball with, and an awful envy and maybe contempt for how he'd turned out. Could be even simpler than that. Maybe he just hated him because he made love to so many women in Mustard that Colby wanted for himself. It's probably silly, but I think Colby always wanted Lou's wife, Jackie, and it killed him that Lou didn't appreciate her and kept chasing after every skirt in town."

"You think Colby could've killed him?"

"Well, sure, he could have. From everything I heard and saw Colby was awfully good with his hands and sometimes I noticed there was an awful coldness about him. It's not hard to believe he'd have it in him to do such a killing. It seems like it was done with a combination of deliberate skill and deep passion."

"You've thought about it a lot."

"Yes, I admit it. It might've been done by Fred Hicks, too. Half the town thinks he's simple because his parents weren't exactly brilliant, and certainly I don't think he's smart, but like Colby he's a man with a lot of hate against authority and I think that gets magnified when the authority's abused. From all I heard, I think Fred was desperately in love with that silly twit Mae Olson and blamed Lou for her running away."

"Did you know Doc Pelham?"

"Met him once. An icicle. One of those snotty men that look a woman over, stripping her with his eyes, while pretending he's miles above all that. He wouldn't dirty his hands on a man like Lou, whatever the provocation."

"You heard Lou'd been messing with the doctor's wife?"

"Oh, yes. Colby told me. I got most of my gossip from Colby. He was very compulsive. He could tell I was interested in everything about the town and he went out of his way to give me every scrap of gossip. I couldn't help feeling sorry for him—I think he sensed that and couldn't decide whether to appreciate it or hate me for it."

23

I WALKED AMELIA the four blocks to a duplex where she lived upstairs and before saying good-night, asked if she happened to know if Mae Olson was in Aberdeen.

"I'm not the kind to keep track of her type. I suppose if she is in town she's waiting tables in some cheap dive where I'd never go."

I thanked her for talking with me and set off to find Wes Fox and Mick Dupree.

The address Dahlberg had given me for Wes was a house not much bigger than a garage that stood next to a vacant corner lot covered with weeds and lined with elms. The inside door was open offering a view through the screen into a living room darkened by drawn shades. When I knocked a redheaded figure appeared in a door straight back and moved my way.

"Well," said Wes, "the intrepid Mustard cop has tracked me to my hideout. You found a witness that claims I was the cop chopper?"

"Is Mick here?" I asked.

I couldn't see his face clearly enough to catch the change of expression but his voice abruptly lost its kidding tone.

"Why'd you want him?"

"Wanted to talk with you both. You going to invite me in?"

I saw his quick grin. "I don't know—next thing you'll be expecting me to offer you a drink."

But he pushed the screen open and stepped aside so I could move past and inside.

The place was furnished with reject furniture and the clutter you'd expect from a couple juveniles. A *Film Fun* magazine lay on the floor beside an easy chair and a *Saturday Evening Post* was on the battered couch. Mick appeared in the doorway, which I guessed was to the kitchen.

"I catch you eating supper?" I asked.

"Is that illegal now?" Wes asked with mock alarm.

"Depends on what you were eating. Go ahead and finish up, I'll just search the room for an ax or hatchet."

Wes's face was blank for a second and I couldn't tell whether he was startled or simply not used to getting kidded back. He recovered, grinned, and said they were just having coffee and they'd bring it out and let me watch because there was none to spare. He added I was welcome to search for anything but stolen women's underwear and unused rubbers.

I sat on the easy chair, they parked on the couch with their coffee cups and watched me between sips. I concentrated on Mick. He looked nervous.

"I've been wondering who was covering for who at your mother's place," I said. "It was plain you two weren't home together the night your father got killed. I don't figure either of you killed him, but wonder what the hell's got you spooked into giving me this hokey story of being together at home that night."

"You don't have to answer him," said Wes, trying to sound casual.

"I got nothing to hide," said Mick. "Ma was just scared because I wasn't home and she thought you'd be suspicious."

"Where were you?"

"Here, in town."

"Why'd that worry her?"

"Well, I don't think she believed I was here. I been sort of involved with a woman and didn't want Ma to know."

"So you lied to me up in your room?"

"Yeah."

For just a second I had the notion the woman might be Amelia, and then rejected it as too wild. My second hunch at first seemed just as dumb but I didn't have anything else to work on so I gave it a try.

"I suppose it was Mae Olson."

His mouth didn't open and his eyes didn't pop; he just stared at me. Wes laughed.

"What's funny?" I asked.

"Well, hell, Mae Olson's old enough to be Mick's mother. What gave you that dumb idea?"

I smiled at him. "Dumb ideas come to me all the time. How well did you know Mae?"

"I knew her when she was a waitress in Mustard. At Nordstrom's. Everybody knew Mae. Not necessarily in the biblical sense."

"Too old for you, huh?"

"Damn few get too old for me that way."

"Where's she working here?"

He laughed again. "You're a great one for trying to tip a man off balance with cute questions, aren't you? I'm supposed to say, 'Gee, Officer, how'd I know?' Right?"

"You might."

"Not me. She works at Bureaugard's, right downtown. Been there near a year."

"You go there a lot?"

"Sure thing. They've got this loose hamburger that's the nuts. All messy and juicy with great pickles. You'd ought to drop around and try them."

"You tried 'em?" I asked Mick.

He looked at Wes, who grinned encouragingly, and then nodded.

I thanked them, left, found a telephone book in a drugstore phone booth, got the Bureaugard address, and went over to the café.

There were two waitresses, one older and broader than my ma, the other built to raise appetites having nothing to do with hamburger. Above the body was a good face framed with brown hair cut short and plain. The lipstick was on too thick but at least she hadn't gone nuts with rouge. There were a couple customers at tables near the front window and an old man at the counter in front of the body. I sat next to him, smiled at her, and said, "Hi, Mae."

She looked at me suspiciously.

"Am I supposed to know you?"

"Nope. We just know some of the same people."

"Like who?"

"Well, there's Wes Fox and Mick Dupree, for starters. And I've been learning some about another fellow you used to know. Mick's pa, Lou."

Not even the last name brought a reaction that'd tell me anything. She asked if I wanted to order.

"No thanks. You know about Lou?"

"I heard."

"Who you think did it?"

She took a deep breath and said it was more than likely done by a committee.

"I understand you and Lou were cozy once and he dropped you."

"That's what you heard?"

"Uh-huh."

"You got it wrong, I did the dropping. He was not a nice guy, you know. It didn't take more than two months for me to figure that out. Actually it was like one night. But he was a hard man to put off. If you think I killed him, think again. I was here in Aberdeen the night he was killed and I can prove it."

"Who were you with, Mick?"

This time she looked startled. "How'd you know that?"

"Talked with him less than an hour ago. He didn't name you, but he says he was with someone in Aberdeen and it seems to figure. He wasn't too crazy about his old man and I just got a hunch that maybe he looked you up and wanted to trade Lou stories and maybe even find a way to make amends."

She glanced self-consciously at the old man sitting beside me. He hadn't looked up since we began talking, had finished his meal and was drinking coffee slowly. When we were both silent for a few seconds he raised his head and waved at his cup. She refilled it, he nodded, added three spoonfuls of sugar, and worked his spoon on it.

Two more customers came in, took a table, and the other waitress went to serve them.

"Look," said Mae, "I'll be off at ten. I'll talk to you then, okay?"

I said that was peachy, I'd be back.

24

WHEN I ENTERED the café Wes Fox and Mick Dupree were sitting at the counter. Both watched my approach and Mae came from the kitchen and stood behind the counter, frowning.

I took the stool on Wes's left and looked them all over.

"The boys don't think I should talk with you," she said.

"Why not?"

"Well, you're not an Aberdeen cop so I don't have to, and you've been hired to find who did Lou so you might not much care who gets blamed as long as you get credit for pinning it on somebody."

"You figure it's that easy to frame somebody for murder?"

"Just say we don't want to take any chances," said Wes.

I gave him my squinty-eyed scowl. It's never scared anybody I can remember but I keep trying it.

"In the army they'd call you a guardhouse lawyer," I said.

"No kidding? I bet you were in the army during the Great War, huh? Probably got a medal for outstanding conduct working on KP, right?"

He had me there. The only thing I ever won was six weeks in the stockade for assaulting an MP in Paris.

"Okay," I said, "so you'd all be nice and comfortable if I go get an Aberdeen cop and we take you downtown for questioning—you think that'd be cozier?"

Wes gave me a tolerant grin. "I don't think you can manage it, old soldier."

"I might not tonight," I admitted, "but tomorrow I can. You rather I came around to where you work in the morning with Officer Dahlberg, and we just haul you downtown for questioning?"

He grinned but Mae wasn't amused.

"Let's talk to him tonight," she said. "If cops pick you up at work your boss'll have kittens and might fire you. And I sure don't want to be pulled out of bed early for questioning."

She cleared away the cups her friends had been using, puttered a few moments in the kitchen, turned out the lights, and we trooped out the front door and watched her lock up.

The town was quiet as we strolled along the deserted street. Mae walked beside me, the two guys partnered behind us.

"I think," I said, "it'd be better if your chums got lost."

"Nothing doing," said Wes.

"What do you want to ask me about?" asked Mae.

"Your husband, Fred, what went on between you and Lou—"

"You want to know about fast Freddie?" said Wes. "I can tell you about him. Like how come he was the fastest man in Mustard. It was simple. He ate lots of beans, you know? It made him fart like crazy and he learned to fart on call so every time he ran a step he'd let one go and he was like rocket propelled. Nobody could keep up and any that tried got gassed so he won every race—"

Mae stopped and turned to him.

"Why don't you guys go on home?"

"Hey, you wanted backup," complained Wes.

"I changed my mind. Go on."

Wes wanted to argue but Mae faced him down, made reassuring noises at Mick, and finally the two guys drifted off, Wes looking sulky, Mick rejected.

Mae watched them moving on and shook her heard.

"They're good kids," she said, "but who likes kids? Look, I need a drink. We'll go to my place but watch yourself because I live in a duplex and if I holler there'll be help, you understand?"

I said she had nothing to worry about and we turned left at the next corner, went to the middle of the block, entered a vestibule, climbed an angled flight of steps, and went into a small apartment with her leading the way turning on lights.

The place was neat and bare with a daybed that had three square pillows leaning against the wall to make it look like a couch but she had spoiled the effect by making it up with blankets neatly spread and tucked. There was a wicker rocking chair and a small table against the wall with chairs on each side and a vase in the center with no flowers. The floor was covered by about the biggest woven rag rug I'd ever seen.

She walked through to a combination kitchen/dining room not much bigger than a cell in the Corden jail. I followed to the door and leaned against the jamb while she pulled a bottle of whiskey from a wall cabinet, chipped ice from the chunk in the top of her dinky icebox, and made drinks in tall glasses.

"How much water?" she asked.

"Halfway."

She handed me the glass and we moved back into the living room.

"I don't think anything I can tell you's going to do you one bit of good," she said.

"Well, it won't do either of us any harm. I hear you were popular in high school."

"That's not what you heard. Everybody's told you I was easy, right?"

"I understand nobody was sure who planted the baby."

"I knew."

"How come?"

"Because Lou was the only one who went all the way without pulling out or using a rubber. I may've been silly and overeager, but I was never just stupid."

"Why didn't you make him use a rubber?"

"Because he was stronger. He never got another chance but one was enough to do me."

"How come you married Fred?"

"He was the only one wanted me bad enough to marry me knocked up. And the fact he really was crazy about me made it seem okay at the time."

"Why'd you leave him?"

"Oh, God, lots of reasons. He was eager as hell but he was also boring. I liked him, if it'd been possible I'd have kept him as a pet, but you can't do that with guys. And soon as I was slim again, Lou started coming around and I knew sooner or later Fred was going to get bad hurt and it seemed better just to get out and hope Fred would find somebody else. . . ."

"What about the guy you ran off with?"

"He was a nothing. He paid my way, I paid him back with what I had, and we split in California. I figured if Fred blamed Benny, the boy I left with, for my running off, maybe he wouldn't get in trouble trying to kill Lou."

"He ever threatened to do that?"

"No."

She said that a little too strong but I didn't push.

"You involved now with Fox?"

"No, I never messed with him."

"How about Mick?"

She blushed. "Mick's something else. It sounds crazy, but I can't help what I feel for him. It's like Lou hurt us both and we need each other against him."

"How'd you meet Mick?"

She looked at her glass and got up. "You want another?"

"Still working on this one."

"I need another."

She went into the kitchen and a moment later was back with her glass half full. I didn't think there was any water in it.

"All right. Where were we?"

"Mick."

"Oh, yeah. Well, Wes brought him around to the café. I found out later Mick had asked him to when they were talking once and Wes mentioned I was in town."

She drank some of her whiskey.

"I guess you maybe heard how Lou beat up on Wes a few years back?"

I nodded.

"That nagged on Wes. I probably shouldn't tell you this but you've probably heard it from others."

"Did Mick ever talk about his old man when he was with you?" I asked.

"Yeah. He said if he knew his son was making love with me he'd probably go nuts."

"You never told him?"

"Of course not."

"Does Fred know?"

"How'd he know?"

"I've never been able to figure out how everybody seems to know about everything in small towns. Maybe the flies pass gossip on."

She held on to her glass with both hands. "My God, it'd be awful if he had found out. . . ."

"Who does know, besides Wes?"

She stared at me.

"Are you trying to tell me something?" she whispered.

"No. I'm just trying to find out all I can."

"I don't want to talk anymore," she said and got to her feet. "Please go."

"Sure," I said, and left.

I still hadn't finished my drink.

25

THE NIGHT WAS changing. West winds moaned through the tall elms and crowded sun-warmed air out. I'd parked the Model T in front of a hotel earlier and walked to each of my meetings, now I hiked back that way. Centerlights at crossroads made light islands every block but in between it was dark and through openings in the foliage above, a quarter moon showed, sailing on its back, like a child-drawn canoe moving through thin clouds that only blurred it. A car engine came to life to my right as I approached a crossing but no lights came on and I guessed a rural Romeo was trying to cop a last feel before his Juliet went in.

The engine revved easy as I neared the corner, watching from the corner of my eye and expecting the lights to come on. When I stepped off the curb and headed for the opposite corner the motor roared, tires scrabbled in the gravel, and the car raced my way. I took off, did a high dive across the curb, tucked sharp, landed on my right shoulder just shy of the sidewalk, and rolled toward the nearest cottonwood.

The car roared by behind me and shot down the street, driven hard and without lights so all that showed was its dark rear end and then it was gone.

I got up and started running for Wes's dinky house. There was no car in front and no sign of a garage out back. Puffing from the run, I circled the block and found nothing like what had chased me, which I figured was a big old Buick.

A walk around the house only showed there were no lights on inside. I went back in front and sat on the stoop.

When I was about to roll a second cigarette two guys came strolling along from the west. The still rising moon left me in shadows and they didn't spot me until just before they turned in on the walk. Bright moonlight showed Wes's hand grip Mick's arm and they slowed for two steps. Then Wes let go and they came on.

"What's the matter?" asked Wes as they neared me. "Wouldn't they let you in a hotel?"

"Where's your car?" I asked.

"Who said I had one?"

"I saw you in it last night."

"That's Ella's. She makes me drive so I can't cop feelies."

"How'd you get to Aberdeen?" I asked Mick.

"Bus."

"Why're you asking about cars?" asked Wes.

"Somebody tried to run me down when I left Mae's place. You're the only guys around who knew I might be there."

"Was it a green Chevy?"

"No. Looked like a Buick."

"So why you giving us grief? We haven't got a Buick, have we, Mick?"

"Where've you two been since Mae sent you off?"

"Just walking and talking about women's ways."

"Where'd that get you?"

"No place. Just like any talk men have about women. You know the difference between a duck?"

"I got a feeling you're going to tell me."

"Each leg is both the same. You know why is a mouse when it spins?"

"I don't give a damn."

"The higher it spins the much."

"Where'd you guys walk?"

"Down by Garfield School. It's beautiful by moonlight. All that brick and those windows with little paper dealies the kiddies cut out and their teacher hangs up. It reaches me deep inside."

"If I find out you tried to run me down, I'll reach you deep inside, believe me."

"Hey, I wouldn't do anything like that, even if I had a Buick. I like you, you're a good listener."

"What'd you do when Lou caught you undressing his cousin?"

"Oh, man, why bring that up? It was the lowest moment in my life, believe me. Lou was not a good listener. He asked a lot of questions but already knew the answers and gave them to you. I mean, you open a car door and find a guy with a nice girl who got a little too warm to keep her blouse on and somewhere along the line lost her bra, would you ask, 'What the hell're you doing?' of the guy who was enjoying the sights and feelings? You think with that going on I was in shape to take him on? Hell, I was so big I got my tool caught in the steering wheel and he had me helpless. He hauled me out and I couldn't manage anything because my pants were down to my knees. It was embarrassing not to mention awkward. Lettie never took me seriously after that. Her hero, bumbling about the gravel with this dumb cop trying to kill him and him busy trying to pull his pants up over a hard-on."

"You want me to believe you found all that was funny?"

"Well, I missed the finer points of it at the moment—a guy like Lou trying to knock your block off is distracting. All I could think of was survival and I managed that by rolling under the car. I'll tell you, it didn't do my best pants any good. Lucky I'd lost the hard-on by then and didn't get it stuck in the transmission or anything. At the start if I'd been thinking I could've pole-vaulted over the car. . . ."

I gave up and left him still reminiscing.

26

IN THE MORNING, after checking out of the hotel, I visited Dahlberg at the police station. He took in my account of talks with Amelia, Mae, Wes, and Mick, enjoyed Wes's story of his aborted romance a little more than seemed proper for a cop, and got really interested about the attempt to run me down.

"Hold on," he said when I described the little I saw of the car, "I'll be right back."

"We had a report on a stolen car last night," he told me as he returned. "Guess the make and color."

"Black Buick?"

"You got it. And it came from a garage two blocks south of where your two buddies hang out."

"Been found?"

"Uh-huh. Two blocks west of their place. You sit tight, we'll pick them up and have a little talk."

The cop who knew Blossom, Wes's boss, went around to the house where Wes was working and got him. Dahlberg picked up Mick at Wes's house. They were kept apart, fingerprinted, and the questioning began with Mick. I just listened at the beginning.

Dahlberg opened with the Dutch uncle line, criticizing Mick for the company he kept, endangering his dead father's reputation, and disappointing his loving mother. Mick watched him sullenly, answering only when crowded, and generally avoided my eyes. Finally Dahlberg switched tactics and said he realized Mick was probably just going along with a guy he liked who'd been trying to help him out.

"The thing you've got to do," said Dahlberg, "is use your head. Just tell the truth and you won't be in any trouble. Carl tells me you're a smart kid with a good future and he doesn't just jabber to hear himself. Now, this business last night—that was Fox's idea, wasn't it? He was getting jittery about Carl's line of questions and threatening to get him in trouble with his boss by hauling him to the police station. So when he decided to borrow a neighbor's car and throw a scare into Carl, you figured you had to go along because you're his buddy, right?"

"No, that's not right. No such thing."

Dahlberg turned tough

"Oh, you mean it was your idea—because you were scared Carl was onto you and the only thing to do was kill him?"

"I don't mean any such thing. I got nothing to be afraid of."

"You're wrong, sonny. You got a whole lot to be afraid of. You got enough to be scared shitless. Let me lay it out. You two guys're the only ones who knew Wilcox was at Mae's place last night. The car used was swiped from a garage right near Fox's place, and left just two blocks from there. We've checked the car for prints. Guess what? Yours and Fox's show up."

"I don't believe it."

"Okay, I lied a little. Fox wiped his prints off the steering wheel and the door handle, you cleaned off yours. But while you were waiting for Carl to come out of Mae's place, your buddy smoked a couple cigarettes and was dumb enough to leave the butts in the ashtray. With fingerprints. Now you want to quit bullshitting and tell what happened?"

For the first time he looked scared, but still shook his head.

"One of the things you got to keep in mind," I told Mick, "is that you and Wes have the best reasons for killing your dad."

"Wes doesn't either. He never held it against Dad that he beat him up for petting with the cousin. Heck, he thought the whole thing was funny, you heard him—"

"I heard his story and I know he's cute enough to make it funny as he could so nobody'd suspect. But how about you? What's bothering me is this killing happened not long after you started getting acquainted with Mae Olson, who was one of your dad's girlfriends. One he said he dropped, and she claimed she quit him. If she did quit him, and he found out you were getting cozy with her, he'd have been madder than a tail-hung cat. It doesn't seem too unlikely he got nasty with her, she told you about it, and you decided the only way she could be protected from him was if he were dead—and you did the job."

He shook his head harder and started sweating.

"Wes took you around to meet Mae, didn't he?" pressed Dahlberg. "It ever dawn on you what a big kick he'd get out of you getting involved with a twitchy your old man laid but couldn't lay again?"

Mick stared beyond us. His head still shook. He tried to speak, couldn't make it and finally took a deep breath.

"I'll admit we took the car and tried to scare you—but that's all. I didn't want Ma to know what'd been going on. I never figured on killing you, no more than Wes did—we just had to try to scare you because there wasn't anything else we could think of and we had to do something. Wes can't help doing stuff like that. He wouldn't have run over you. He'd heard how fast you are and he said it'd be fun to see how you'd jump and afterwards he couldn't stop laughing at the way you dove across the curb and did that roll—"

It took a lot longer when we talked with Wes before he admitted what Mick said was true but at last he accepted blame for the idea and insisted it was more of a practical joke than anything. After putting Wes back in a cell, Dahlberg and I generally agreed they were leveling with us.

He went over to Mae's, found her having late breakfast, and Dahlberg told her we had a big problem and needed to talk with her awhile. She wasn't exactly tickled pink but said sure, invited us in, and gave us coffee.

She denied that Lou knew anything about his son's interest in her and tried to make us believe even that had been innocent.

"So okay, I've let him fool around some but we're not having an affair—he's too young for me. It's just that he needed help and I could tell what he'd gone through with Lou and just couldn't turn my back on him."

"What made you think he needed help?" I asked.

"Well, for heaven's sake, he was Lou Dupree's kid, of course he needed help."

"Tell us about the first time he came to see you in Aberdeen."

"Well, it started with Wes. I spotted this redhead at the counter looking at the menu on the wall. I thought he looked familiar and asked if he came from Mustard and at first he pretended he was surprised I'd guess that but pretty soon grinned and called me by name and said he remembered me from when I worked in Nordstrom's. We talked some and I liked it that he didn't say anything about Lou because it seemed likely he'd heard about us."

Mae had crinkly eyes, pale lashes, and thin-lipped mouth. Her cheeks were broad and almost flat. Her look was direct, even pushy. When she talked the stare never wavered and you could almost hear a click when she switched her attention from me to Dahlberg, depending on who'd asked the last question.

"How long after that first time was it before he brought Mick around?" asked Dahlberg.

"About a month."

"Was it a surprise?"

"No. He'd said I ought to meet him. I mean, after Wes had been showing up pretty regular we got talking enough so Lou did get mentioned. It was kind of involved—Wes has a way of showing real interest in a person, you know? He asked how come I left Mustard when I did, and how come the business with the guy I left with didn't last. Wes can poke into stuff like that without seeming nosy, just honestly interested. And then he said the reason he asked was, he was pals with Mick, Lou's son, and he'd learned what a bastard Lou was as a father and he figured he'd been mean to me and he thought I should know Mick because Mick was really a very lonely guy and afraid of women. So I said bring him around."

"How'd he act?"

"Like a kid scared of women. He got to me right off. His face isn't all sharp and tight like Lou's, it's softer and broader and real nice. And his eyes glow when he looks at me."

"You get any time alone with him?"

"Oh, sure. The first time Wes brought him around he said he had to go meet somebody and Mick walked me home. I thought we'd probably talk about his dad a lot but we didn't. Not at first. Mick was only in town Saturday nights back then and got in the habit of walking me home and I'd invite him in and we drank coffee and talked and finally I kissed him and he took to it real quick. That's all it came to, though. I mean, some kissing and hugging. He never tried anything and it was awfully sweet."

I could see that kind of talk made Dahlberg uncomfortable and pretty soon he leaned across the table and asked, "When did Lou find out his kid was seeing you?"

"What makes you think he did?"

"Haven't you figured out that's why Wes Fox brought the kid around to meet you? You forgotten the beating Lou gave Wes a few years back? You think Wes ever forgot it?"

"Well, I didn't think about that. . . ."

"You thought old Wes was just playing Dan Cupid, huh?"

"What're you trying to say?"

"That Wes brought Mick around, figuring something might come of it, and when it did, he let the word get back to Lou that his kid was making out where Lou'd been dumped. Wes'd think that was funnier than hell, and he hoped it'd make fireworks. Now what we got to figure out was what brought on the murder. The way I figure it, Lou burned, got in touch with Mick, and told him to come around. Mick guessed what he wanted to see him about and showed up at his room, carrying a hatchet along, hidden somehow, and when they clashed, went to work."

Mae's crinkly eyes popped some as she turned to me.

"This guy's crazy. If Mick went into Lou's room carrying a hatchet, you think Lou'd just lay there on his bunk in his B.V.D.'s while the boy hacked away?"

Dahlberg straightened up. "So maybe he sneaked in, found Lou asleep, and had at him."

"That's stupid. Mick's not that kind of boy and Lou wasn't the kind of guy who falls asleep early Sunday night."

"When he'd been drinking with no supper?"

"Who said he'd been drinking?"

"Doc Pelham."

Mae raised her eyebrows.

"You know what Doc Pelham thought of Lou?"

"Tell me," said Dahlberg.

"He hated his guts. He'd be glad to claim Lou died drunk."

Dahlberg looked solemn, almost thoughtful. "Where were you that Sunday night?"

"I was home and Mick was with me. Okay?"

"So you cover for each other. I don't suppose Wes was at your place too?"

She turned red. "You really are a bastard, aren't you? No

he wasn't here. He's never been in my house or in my pants. Now how'd you like to get the hell out?"

Dahlberg nodded, got up, and looked at me.

I looked at Mae.

"Will you talk with me a little more?" I asked. "I really don't think Mick did the job, but we've got to get all the story straight and so far it's just not working out."

"I'll talk to you, but not him."

Dahlberg shrugged and walked out through the front.

"Got any more coffee?" I asked.

She got up. "I'll make another pot."

27

MAE WATCHED ME roll a smoke and when I offered, took it. I rolled another, lit both, and we puffed a few seconds. Her eyes with their crinkly edges were steady and studying.

"Okay," I said, "let's lay it out flat—I can't believe you're the kind of woman who'd act like a high school sophomore with a grown boy just because he's younger. If Mick was with you Sunday night long enough to give him an alibi, don't tell me you were holding hands all night."

She scowled. "What do you want, juicy details?"

"Tell me what really happened and make me believe it."

"All right. Yes, we slept together and we did that after doing what you do to get sleepiest. Satisfied?"

"It still sounds like you're only giving him an alibi."

"You've just got to get it all, don't you? If you have to know, he was awkward and too quick and embarrassed to tears but we worked it out and when he went to sleep he was happy and he was still happy in the morning."

"Did he talk about his old man?"

"Yes. Right after he came too soon and bawled. He said he bet his dad hadn't done that and I told him the hell he didn't—he came the minute he got in and without ever so much as trying to make it good for me, which Mick had. I told him he was twice the man his father was and bigger in the bargain. That was only a little lie but it made him happy. I even laid out how his dad forced me in a car out by a windbreak on the prairie near a deserted farm. That was true all the way. If I'd had an ax along I'd have used it, given the chance. I hated him ever after but never thought of murder."

I took all that in, watching her close. She squirmed a little and scowled defiantly.

"Well? Don't you believe me?"

"You're telling me the first time Mick got into you was the night Lou got chopped—maybe at the same time?"

"That's what I said, haven't you been listening?"

"Yeah. It was handy as hell."

"I think it was perfect."

"Where was Fox that night?"

She shrugged. "Somehow I never got around to ask."

"You know of anything happening that might've got him worked up to go kill Lou while you two were having your party?"

"Like what?"

"If he knew Mick was actually with you—he might've got the notion to tip Lou off. I think that'd given him a lot of satisfaction."

She stared at me with an expression I couldn't read; she might have been wondering what the hell gave me such a fiendish idea, or maybe she suddenly realized I might be right. After a second she shook her head.

"No. And I'm not saying that just because I won't believe he's the stinker you think. The fact is, Lou went after him like a maniac the night he caught him with the cousin. Wes was positive he was going to get killed and he stayed scared of him until he was dead. Anyway, if Wes had told Lou, Lou'd have come straight after the two of us."

"So maybe Wes was scared enough to figure if he didn't kill Lou, his own ass would be in a sling when the man found out he'd brought you and Mick together."

She looked doubtful. "I can't imagine Lou just laying on his bunk naked if Wes came around. Unless he was drunk asleep. . . ."

"He must've been."

She frowned and got to her feet.

"I don't know—I can't imagine Wes doing it."

That didn't come out with as much sureness as she wanted and she got a worried look, shook her head, and said she had to go over to the restaurant and start getting things ready for the lunch crowd. We walked side by side in silence until we were in front of the café and stopped a moment, squinting against the bright sun that reflected off the windows. She shaded her eyes with one hand, looking up at me.

"You think you can convince that other cop that Mick didn't kill Lou?"

"Probably."

"So you believe me about Mick?"

"Yeah. I think he's a lucky kid at the moment."

"It won't last. Pretty soon he'll look around and see all the girls his age and wonder what the hell he's doing with me."

"Mae, you're not ready for the cane and rocking chair for quite a while. And younger girls'll seem like root beer after you."

My grin didn't get one back. She lowered her head and dropped her hand to her side as she stared at the café door. "It won't last," she said. "I felt sorry for him and he needed me. It made a good match for a while, but they all burn out quick, right? Good-bye."

Dahlberg took my report in without comment and it was a relief dealing with a cop who didn't think he had to be a hardnose all the time. It was a little surprising when he even seemed to accept Mae's notions about Wes Fox.

"Looks like you got yourself down to Doc Pelham, Colby

Link, or that Hicks guy," he said. "If it's Pelham, I'd guess you're out of luck."

"The next thing," I said, "is find the damned weapon. I think it's a hatchet. And any damned body might have one. If it was Lou's, there'd been no reason to carry it off."

"A guy commits murder, he doesn't always think cool after. More'n likely he's scared silly."

"Whoever did this one, did it deliberate and steady. The hits were too perfect. It was done by somebody who'd been thinking of it a long time and wanted to do it just right."

"A genius killer, huh?"

"Or a simple-minded one. Who didn't get all fussed about what might go wrong, just figured the way to go at it and didn't throw in complications."

"A guy like Colby Link?"

"Or Fred Hicks."

"Well, happy hatchet hunting."

I started to go and remembered something.

"You talk to the owner of the Buick Wes borrowed?" I asked.

"Yeah. Old dude named Isakson. Told me he always left the keys in the car because if he didn't he couldn't find them when he wanted to drive."

"Where was the car?"

"In front of his house, like always."

I thanked him, cranked up the Model T, and headed back to Mustard.

28

I SPENT MOST of the drive trying to imagine ingenious places somebody might hide a hatchet, while thinking it was most likely thrown in a field, the swimming hole, a passing boxcar, or simply dumped back in the killer's basement with other tools.

My first stop in Mustard was the mayor's office in City Hall. He welcomed me with restraint shy of enthusiasm.

"What've you accomplished?" he asked, letting me know he wouldn't believe it was worth the trip no matter the answer.

"I crossed off three suspects."

"Just like that?"

"Right. What I need is your help in getting a search started for the murder weapon. A hatchet."

"You had to go to Aberdeen to figure that out?"

"If the murderer was in Aberdeen, that'd been one place to look for the hatchet. Since now I don't think anybody there did it, we can narrow down to Mustard."

"You'll need search warrants, it'll take forever."

"Not if we convince everybody they'd be helping solve this thing."

"How do you manage that?"

"First we get Pastor Skogslund to join us. We search your place and his to set the example, and move on."

For a couple seconds, as he glared, I thought I'd blown it, then he shook his head in wonder and said I had the damnedest gall of any man he'd met.

"If you go along," I said, "who else can say no?"

"And the pastor's presence will sanctify the whole business. You're something, Wilcox. I'm not quite sure what but it doesn't matter. All right, let's go see Skogslund."

The pastor was delighted and suggested we start with a look through his home. The mayor made polite noises about that being unnecessary but agreed to go along in a manner that suggested he was humoring us.

We found no hatchet, only an old ax so rusty it obviously hadn't been used since about the time of Columbus's landing. We then trooped over to the mayor's house where he led us to his basement and pointed out the hatchet hung on a wall rack with his saw, hammer, and other tools. It was the claw type with a hammer head on one side and a sharp, oiled blade on the other. If the mayor had used it recently it was plain he'd cleaned it carefully before hanging it up. It shook him bad when I asked if he'd mind our taking it for a check against the hatchet marks in the victim. He stared at me, then at the pastor, and finally said go ahead.

After that he didn't quibble when I suggested a visit to Doc Pelham's place. Frances answered our ring, gawked at us with appropriate wonder, and listened with eyes wide and lips parted as the mayor explained what was going on.

"There's no compulsion here," he assured her. "No search warrant—we're simply asking responsible citizens to cooperate in this effort to eliminate all possible persons with a concern in the case from any hint of suspicion. . . ."

"Oh, dear," said Frances, "I'll have to ask The Doctor. Please wait here—"

She scuttled off and a few moments later returned, looking flushed and frightened.

"He's coming," she said. "I'm not to let you in until he arrives. Could you just wait—"

"Of course," said Pastor Skogslund, " don't you worry your head a bit. We understand."

Within three minutes Doc showed up in his black Packard, parked precisely before his front walk, got out of the car, and walked grimly to the porch. I guessed he'd worked hard from the moment of dialogue with his wife until he arrived before us, getting his temper reined in. He ignored the pastor and me as he scowled at the mayor.

"I don't imagine this was your idea," he said.

"Doc, the three of us have already been to Pastor Skogslund's house and my place where we checked the premises for a hatchet. Officer Wilcox has mine in the trunk of our car and I have agreed to permit an examination to determine whether or not it could be the murder weapon—"

He went on to repeat what he'd said to Frances while the doctor stared at him with a look somewhere between scorn and wonder. When the mayor ran down Doc's eyes moved to the pastor and finally me.

"This is your cute approach, isn't it? But aren't you overlooking something?"

"You mean the fact you did the exam? No. We'll have somebody else double-check your work."

A quick glance at the mayor told the doc this came as a shock to him. Doc Pelham almost smiled.

"You're going to have the body disinterred?"

"Doesn't it figure?"

The grim expression returned. "Of course," he said.

"All right, let's get through this charade."

His hatchet, which was laying on a bench near the furnace room, was the broad style, with a pounding edge but no nail puller. It had rust along the blade I didn't think would show if it'd been recently used and cleaned. I said as much but asked it, for the record, we could take it along for checking.

"Be my guest."

He didn't look worried but I had a feeling he wouldn't have been even if we'd found fresh blood on the thing.

Neither Link or Hicks admitted to owning a hatchet but welcomed a search through their junk to confirm it.

By the time we finished with them it was near six o'clock and the mayor wanted a break for dinner. I said we should check Dupree's place first since news of the search was bound to spread and it wouldn't be a great idea to have anyone forewarned. The pastor backed me up and Mayor Tollefson reluctantly went along.

It surprised me when Mick answered the Dupree door.

"When'd you get back?" I asked.

"A while ago—why?"

The mayor took over and explained our visit and what had happened so far. In the midst of that, Jackie appeared and so he went back and gave her the whole line. She actually smiled and said how clever and told us to look wherever we wished.

I asked Mick if he had a Boy Scout hatchet. He said he did once but gave it away when he outgrew scouting three or four years back. He didn't remember who he gave it to.

We could find no hatchet in the house.

Pastor Skogslund, the mayor, and I sat in Tollefson's car, reviewing the searches and considering next moves. I suggested we try Aunt Leck's.

"Why?" asked Pastor Skogslund.

"A couple reasons. One I can't think of anyplace else, and two, we know Lou'd been trying to move in on the schoolteacher and I'd like a look at her room. You got any better ideas?"

He didn't and neither did the mayor.

I think Aunt Leck would have turned down the approach flat

if we hadn't had the pastor along. He easily coaxed her into indulging our dumbness and even went up to Yvette's room and told her what was up.

I couldn't quite figure Yvette's reaction. At first she seemed upset, then she turned sullen, and finally it just struck her as funny. She sat on the bed while I poked around, the pastor talked to her, and the mayor tried to pretend he was watching my snooping but mostly kept watching Yvette with his hot blue eyes.

She had a lot of space for anyone living in a boardinghouse, and even a closet you could step into. The double bed, tucked just behind the entry door on the left as we entered, faced north. On the right an oak desk stood against the south wall and a straight-backed chair faced it. The desk surface was clear except for a stack of books, an inkstand, and penholder. A white bureau squatted against the east wall between the desk and the closet door and a white pitcher and matching washbowl covered half its surface before a large mirror. An upholstered rocking chair filled the northwest corner of the room. Two large windows on the north wall were curtained and draped in white and blue. The bedspread matched the drapes.

I found the closet filled with clothes carefully hung on wire hangers and there were square boxes on the shelf just above eye level. They held hats. Three pairs of shoes stood on the floor in pairs, precisely as a model daughter would place them.

The mayor and pastor kept apologizing all the while I poked about and she kept assuring them it was perfectly all right. When we left I stopped by the door and faced her.

"Does Jackie Dupree ever come around to the library?"

"Why yes, she's been there. I wouldn't say she was a regular."

"When was the last time?"

"A couple weeks ago, I guess—"

"Not long before Lou died?"

She frowned and finally nodded. "Yes. On Saturday."

"How'd she act toward you?"

"All right. I wouldn't say she went out of her way to be friendly, but she wasn't unfriendly either."

I thanked her, and said if it made any difference, I hadn't expected to find a hatchet in her room. She smiled and closed the door.

"Now what?" asked the mayor as we stood out front.

"We'll go look in the library."

He glanced at his watch. "It's after six-thirty. Yvette'll be opening it in less than an hour."

"That's okay, we won't take long. You got a key?"

"Yes."

"Fine. Let's go."

29

"WELL," SAID THE mayor as we entered the library, "where do you begin? Under *H* for hatchet?"

"It'd likely be stuck behind books on a top or bottom shelf—where it wouldn't be noticed unless somebody moved a mess of books at a time."

The mayor looked skeptical. "I can believe someone, and I assume you suspect our librarian, might hide the hatchet temporarily after the murder. But it's hard to believe she'd be dumb enough to just leave it there later when anybody could come in and find it by accident."

"Right. But if it wasn't Yvette and the murderer wanted to hide it quick, this'd be the handiest place, especially since Lou probably had a key the killer could find and use. He might even have figured when it was found cops would figure Yvette did it."

Tollefson didn't look convinced but Pastor Skogslund nodded in agreement, and with a sly grin after a glance at the stacks, suggested he'd start under the *H*s since they were low enough to be in his reach and high enough to save him squatting. The mayor grudgingly agreed to check the lower shelves and I moved the library ladder to the area nearest the door and climbed up.

It seemed most logical the killer would have used the nearest place to the entrance. I started on the left side.

There was nothing but books. Not even any dust.

I came down, moved the ladder to the right side, at the end of the alphabet. The pastor had become distracted by a small volume that looked like poetry and was reading with a saintly expression on his battered face. The mayor was on his knees along the bottom shelves across the room, removing half a dozen books at a time and carefully replacing them, as if he were handling eggs.

The first thing I noticed after climbing up was books in the top corner were closer to the edge than anywhere else. I only pulled out the first two when the hatchet head came in sight.

"Score," I said.

A moment later we gathered around it at the librarian's desk and just then Yvette walked in.

We looked at her and she stared at the hatchet. Then she looked at me.

"It seemed likely the killer hid this in here after using it on Lou," I said.

"Someone with a key," she said. Her voice was husky.

"Which could've been on Lou."

"I heard he was naked."

"His clothes were handy."

"Where'd you find it?" she asked, looking at the small hatchet.

"Top shelf behind you on the right."

She didn't turn to look.

"Now what?"

"We find out if it was really the one used."

"That seems pretty likely, doesn't it? And then you charge me, right?"

"Probably not. We don't have a motive strong enough to make you likely and as the mayor said when we came in, even if you hid it here in a panic after the killing, you wouldn't be dumb enough to leave it there for somebody to stumble on."

We heard someone coming up the stairs and Tollefson quickly asked Yvette if she was too upset to handle patrons. She shook her head.

The pastor offered me his handkerchief to wrap the hatchet handle and we carefully moved out after letting two high school students enter. They were too busy taking to each other to notice the weapon I carried at my side opposite them.

There was a short debate downstairs with Mayor Tollefson before we went back to Doc Pelham's. I said we should ask the doc for his notes on the autopsy and check the measurements record against what we had on hand. The mayor thought that would be pointless if Pelham was still a suspect. I felt it would be interesting to find out what the doc said and Pastor Skogslund said it was worth a try.

Doc Pelham was just north of cordial when the mayor explained what we had in mind. He got out his notes and placed them before us. They were so detailed and thorough it took me a while to find the measurements and a few minutes after that it was plain the Boy Scout hatchet was the tool used, assuming we could trust the doc.

We left Pelham's house and walked slowly west, in the general direction of Tollefson's home.

"It seems to me," said the mayor, pausing on a corner under a streetlight, "that it comes down to Jackie Dupree. She has the strongest motives, having been at odds with Lou for years and was probably sure he'd attack Mick when he found out he was sleeping with Lou's old girlfriend. The hatchet was no doubt available in the house. . . ."

I listened, watching moths, beetles, and other winged maniacs wheeling and batting around the streetlight above.

"Maybe," said Pastor Skogslund, "we should all go home and rest on this. It's getting on and I feel a need to think about it—or perhaps better yet, forget it awhile. I can't quite face the idea of it all anymore this evening."

Tollefson liked that idea and I grabbed it happily.

It just had occurred to me I'd overlooked an obvious detail and felt too dumb about it to let either of them know. We said good night and went our ways.

30

IT WAS JUST past 9:00 P.M. when I called the Dupree house from City Hall and Mick answered.

"Thought you might like to know," I said, "we found your hatchet."

That got me several seconds of silence.

"You want to know where?"

"Well, uh, sure—"

"It was on a top shelf in the library. Hidden behind books."

"How you know it's mine?"

"Well, first it's a Boy Scout hatchet but the big clue is your initials on the handle butt."

"Oh."

"I guess you don't remember yet who you gave it to?"

He took a deep breath. "Actually, I think maybe Dad took it when he moved out. I'm not sure but it seems like it was around till he left."

"You'd been using it regular till then?"

"Well, no, but I'd see it in my closet on the floor there."

"It was used to kill him."

He said oh. I let him stew a few seconds before speaking again.

"You better come over to City Hall and talk. We got several angles to cover.

"Can't it wait till morning?"

"If you don't come here, I'll come over there."

He gave that about two seconds and said no, he guessed it'd be better if he came to see me. He promised to come around in a few minutes.

"Fine. And Mick, don't call Wes first. Or Mae. Come straight. You take time for telephone calls and I'll know."

He didn't ask why I thought he'd be calling anybody and I thought that was interesting.

After about half a minute I went through information to get numbers for Mae and Wes and called both. Neither line was busy.

Mick came in on time to see me hanging up. His face looked frozen and he avoided my eyes.

When he was seated I rolled a smoke, lit it, and let him sit a few seconds.

"Give me a reason why your old man would take your hatchet along when he left home," I said.

He straightened up and managed to meet my strare.

"He liked to take little fishing trips once in a while. He cooked out and used my hatchet to chop kindling. He'd borrowed it quite a few times."

I watched him some more and then smiled, friendly like.

"You probably think I'm pretty dumb because I didn't ask what happened to Wes Fox's alibi for that Sunday night after Mae told me you and she were playing bed games when your dad died. You remember telling me you were with Wes, right? You both told me that. And before that your mother had you for an alibi until you admitted that was a lie. So what it comes down to is nobody's clear—not Mama, Mae, Wes, or you. The four prime suspects. The ones with the great motives and time. So whose ass is most important, next to yours?"

He kept his face stiff but his body twitched and I could practically smell him starting to sweat.

"Well?"

"It was most likely Wes. He could've taken his girlfriend's car and done it."

"She let him use it any old time?"

"Just about."

"You know her telephone number?"

He shook his head.

I picked up the telephone and asked the operator for Ella Parker. The operator said Ella'd still be at the café and Albertson wouldn't appreciate her getting a call there.

"So give me Albertson."

She got him, I identified myself, and said I'd like to talk with his waitress a minute on police business.

"Don't tell me Ella's a suspect."

"I won't. Just get her on the line and leave her alone, okay?"

He said sure and a moment later she said "Hello?"

"This is Wilcox. I've been talking with Mick Dupree and a little problem's come up. The Sunday night Lou Dupree got killed, were you in Aberdeen visiting Wes?"

"When I go to Aberdeen I stay with my folks—I never stayed with Wes."

"Sure. But you understand I'll have to check that with them—you want to give me their number?"

"No. You don't want to bother them, they'll get all upset—"

"You weren't with them that night, right?"

"Oh, God, do you have to go into this? All right, I was with Wes. Are you satisfied?"

"You didn't stay all night, did you?"

"No. I left him about midnight."

"Uh-huh. You sure he didn't ride back to Mustard with you?"

"Of course not. He wouldn't have had any way to get back to Aberdeen for work Monday morning."

"Unless he drove your car back after he killed Lou."

"Oh, come on! Wes wouldn't kill anybody, that's crazy."

"Yeah, I don't really believe it either. But he did have it in for Lou good and you know it. How'd he get it to Lou that his kid was messing with Mae Olson?"

The line hummed awhile before she got around to answer.

"What gave you that idea?"

"Figure it out. People been hating Lou Dupree for years, and all of a sudden somebody kills him. He hadn't done any new girl dirt lately, or laid anybody's wife we've heard of in the last few weeks before he got chopped. So maybe somebody was afraid of what he'd do to Mick—or Mae, if he found out about them getting cozy."

"You're thinking Mick's mother, Jackie?"

"Who'd be more worried about Mick?"

"Nobody, I guess, but maybe Mae. . ."

"Or Mick himself."

"I don't think Mick would've done it like that."

"Actually, the style is the only thing that makes me keep thinking of Wes. He's got this wild sense of humor, you know, the hits, all so exact."

"No. Wes just isn't a violent guy. Not ever. Look, I'll tell you what you're after if you promise not to tell Wes I did."

"You got a deal."

"Wes told Colby Link. He knew Colby'd pass it on."

"Why'd he want that?"

"Oh, hell, that's just Wes. It was a way to get back at Lou for humiliating him that time. I don't think he really believed Lou'd do anything awful and he wanted him to hurt, that's all."

I thanked her, hung up. Mick stared at me, looking beat.

"Did she say Wes told?" he asked.

I nodded. He looked down miserably.

"So it was you, Mae, or your mother. Who did it?"

He lowered his head, shuddered, and then, after a moment, straightened up, leaned back, and met my eyes.

"Okay. I killed him. Now, for God's sake, leave Mae and Ma alone."

31

WHEN MICK WAS properly parked in the cell at the back of City Hall I telephoned the mayor and reported developments.

He wasn't happy about it and wanted to know how I got the confession.

"It was easy—he had the choice of taking the blame himself or seeing his girlfriend or mother nailed for it. Mick's the kind who's honor-bound to protect his women."

"Well, I suppose. . ." His voice faded and then he got brisk. "I think we'd do well to bring Pastor Skogslund back into the picture. I'll be over in a few minutes and will bring him if he's willing."

They showed up in fifteen minutes.

I reviewed the questioning of Mick and in the end the pastor shook his head sadly, saying he just couldn't believe the boy did it.

"Who'd you like for it?"

He sighed, folded his hands tightly in his lap, and gave me a sorrowful smile.

"I want it to have been suicide—or perhaps divine intervention—but one is as unlikely as the other, isn't it?"

"About. What I want to do now is call Jackie and Mae, tell them about the confession, see what they say."

We went around on that for several minutes and at last both agreed.

The moment I spoke to Jackie she asked if Mick was with me and I said yes. She said she was coming over and hung up.

The mayor wanted me to drive to Aberdeen after Mae but I persuaded him to let me call and see if she'd come once she heard of Mick's confession. He reluctantly agreed.

"I'm sorry," I began when Mae came on the line, "but figured you'd ought to know. Mick has confessed to killing Lou."

She took in her breath sharply.

"He says he did it because he was afraid of what his father'd do when he found out you two were sleeping together."

"Where is he?"

"In the cell here."

"Let him out. He's lying to protect me. I did it."

"From Aberdeen?"

"Please, don't try to be funny. Look, I'm coming to Mustard, okay? Will you let me talk to him when I get there?"

"Sure. How'll you come?"

"Never mind—tell him I'm coming. Will you do that?"

"Glad to."

Jackie came in as I was saying good-bye to the dead phone. She looked like she'd aged about twenty years since the last time we talked, and her eyes had the wild glow of a revival minister detailing hell to a guilt-cowed audience.

She hurried to the pastor and grabbed his arms with both hands. "He thinks he's protecting me," she said. "Mick wouldn't kill his father, he's just not made that way."

"You figure he thinks you did it?" I asked.

"It's hard to believe, but he might. He knows how mad I got at Lou and how afraid I was of what he might do if he learned about Mae and Mick."

"How'd you hear Lou knew about them?"

"Lou called me that afternoon to ask what I was going to do about it. At first I couldn't imagine what he was talking about— Mick never mentioned anything about being involved with a woman. Oh, I was suspicious, but honestly, until then I couldn't accept the fact he's grown up now and it'd be natural. Anyway, I told Lou he was an idiot if he thought I was going to slap Mick's hands and tell him to give her up or I'd not let him have desserts."

"What'd he say?"

"He said she was too old for him and Mick might get a disease and if I didn't break it up he damn well would."

"Was Lou drunk when he called?"

"Yes."

"What'd you say you'd do?"

"I said if he did anything to Mick, I'd kill him."

"Jackie," said Pastor Skogslund, "you better talk with a lawyer before you say anything more."

Jackie seemed to shrink and I got her into my chair. After a few seconds she asked if she could talk with her son. I looked at the mayor who looked at the pastor.

"Why not?" said Skogslund.

So I led her back and left them sitting on the cot.

Mae showed up a little after ten. She was wearing the same dress I'd seen her in the last time I visited her café. Her mouth was tight and her eyes were wild.

"Okay," I told her, "I'm going to get Mick and his mother in here and we're going to talk a little. Do us all a favor and keep quiet except when I ask you a question. Will you do that?"

"I already told you I killed Lou. What more do you want?"

"You'll have to prove it. We know you're in love with Mick and figure it's your fault he's made this confession. His mother is with him now—she doesn't know you confessed and I don't want her to know yet."

The wildness left her eyes and I thought I saw hope. She lifted her chin and asked if Mick knew she'd confessed to me.

"No."

"All right, I'll do as you say."

The mayor decided my room was too crowded so after I got Mick and Jackie we moved to the library and sat around the big center table in chairs pulled up close.

I leaned toward Mick. "Tell us how you killed your father. All the details, slow and easy."

"This is nonsense," said Jackie, "keep still until we get a lawyer."

He shook his head.

"How'd you hear that Lou knew you were messing with Mae?" I asked.

"I heard Ma talking to him on the phone."

"When?"

"Saturday."

"You were in Aberdeen, how'd you hear her in Mustard?"

"I guess it was Friday—I get mixed up—"

"When did Lou talk to you?" I asked Jackie.

"Saturday. Mick couldn't have known anything about it."

I looked at Mae.

"When did you find out Lou knew?"

"Saturday. He called me after he called her. That's when I decided I had to kill him."

"You were in bed with Mick Saturday night—how'd you get here to use the hatchet?"

"Mick went to sleep after we made love. He always does, out cold. I just got up, dressed, went down to the old man's house, took his car, and drove here. It only took a little over half an hour. It was oven hot in Lou's room and he was naked on the cot, dead drunk. I had a butcher knife with me but then I saw the hatchet in the corner with his bedroll and I knew if I hit him with that he'd be finished with the first shot. I was so mad at him for abusing Mick and raping me I went crazy-wild. I hit him in the neck first, yelling that's for being such an asshole, and I hit him in the face and said that was for forcing me, and hit him in the belly and then the privates and all my hate was gone and I nearly passed out."

She stopped and sat hunched over and shuddering. Mick got up, went to her, and stood with his hands on her shoulders, staring at us.

"She's just making it up—she couldn't have gone and me not know—"

"What'd you do about the blood?" I asked Mae.

"Oh, God," she said, "it was all over. On me and my clothes . . . the wall and floor. . . I found his spare blanket, took it and spread it on the seat of the car before I got back in. When I got home I took all of my stained clothing and burned it in the furnace the next day along with the blanket. Mrs. Sanders, who owns the duplex and lives downstairs, was visiting her cousin in Iowa so there was nobody to notice the fire in summer."

"What about footprints?"

"I smeared them with my blouse."

"How'd you get here tonight?"

"The old man's Buick, the one I used to come and kill Lou. This time the keys weren't in it but I knew from Schwartz, the car thief, how to jump-start it."

By the time I stopped asking her questions the details were too complete for there to be any doubt. Mick tried but finally Mae told him gently to shut up. The only thing he'd do by trying to prove she hadn't done it was to leave his mother the only possible murderer.

Mick sank to his knees by her chair and she bent over him, stroking his head and shoulders as he bawled.

I looked at Jackie, who watched her son and his lover with an expression I couldn't figure. It almost looked serene.

MD

Adams, Harold,
1923-

The late town cop.

11/76

DATE			

BAKER & TAYLOR